Timeless Captive

Book 6 – Timeless Hearts Series

KAY P. DAWSON

DEDICATION

Thank you to the other wonderful authors in this series for making this so much fun – Sandra E. Sinclair, Anna Rose Leigh & Peggy L. Henderson. I believe we have created a truly timeless series ;)

Kay

Chapter 1

"I'm going to make sure that man pays if it's the last thing I do." Gabe clenched his jaw tight, trying to choke down the fury that was threatening to consume him.

"Well, I just thought you should know. I made a promise to myself I'd find you and let you know before I continued on my way, so I've done my part."

Gabe nodded at the man across from

him. Brody Hayes had worked for a short time with Martin Paine, a man who Gabe hated with a passion. And who he'd just found out had been swindling him on top of everything else he'd done to him.

"So, all those months I was going in and paying off my dead brother's farm for his widow, Martin was letting her believe she still had to pay for it? That man is going to answer to me. I don't know how, or when, but he and I have a score to settle."

Gabe didn't mention to the other man that he was sure Martin was responsible for his brother's death too. And for making everyone around town believe that Gabe himself was a swindler and a thief.

And now he'd just found out, the money he'd been paying for his sister-in-law Elizabeth's farm had been going into the man's own pocket.

Thankfully, Brody mentioned that Elizabeth had remarried, and her new husband had taken care of Martin after he'd been told what was going on. So the farm now belonged to Elizabeth, as it should have long ago.

But it didn't soothe Gabe's anger. Martin Paine had been a thorn in his side for years. He was aptly named.

"What do you plan on doing? I'd be happy to stick around and help you settle things with the man. He owes me a pretty penny too. But I have some things to take care of myself back home, so I have to keep moving." Brody stood and slapped his hat against his leg, a cloud of dust settling in the air around them. He reached down and tipped his glass back. "Thanks for the drink. I'll get the next one when I'm back around these parts."

Gabe stood to shake the man's hand. "Thanks again. I owe you."

Brody started to walk toward the door of the saloon, pushing his hat onto his head. He turned back and tipped his head slightly to one side. "Of course, I might be able to give you some more information to help you out, since I can't stick around myself. I did overhear Martin talking about corresponding with a lady back east about coming out here to marry him. I'd feel awful sorry for that poor girl to get out here and be stuck with a man like him. And I'm pretty sure Martin would be fighting mad to have that woman end up with someone else."

He nodded at Gabe, then turned and left.

Gabe sat back down slowly, leaning back in his chair. He was in the saloon on Maplesville's main street, a town about a half-day's ride from Heartsbridge. He'd been here since his brother died in the mining accident. There had been plenty of rumors around Heartsbridge that Gabe had caused trouble, and in fact should feel responsible for his own brother's death.

Thankfully, an old man who had a farm just outside of town said he didn't care about anyone's past, that he judged a man based on his gut feelings. He'd liked Gabe when they first met, and he'd offered him a job on his farm caring for the livestock and helping with the crops.

Then old man Templeton had gone east for a few months to try and find a doctor who could cure his various ailments, so he'd asked Gabe to look after things in his absence. Gabe had been using his wages to pay Martin Paine for the farm his brother had been owing on when he died. Others may believe Gabe to be a no-good for nothing vagrant, but he wasn't the kind of man to walk out and leave his brother's widow and young nephew destitute.

He'd even thought of marrying her himself to be able to provide for her, but she deserved better than a man like him.

And now it was time to make Martin pay.

He'd been suspicious of the man for months before the mine accident. The company who owned the mine had hired

Martin to be in charge, believing he'd be the best man for the job. Martin owned much of the land around Heartsbridge and was the banker in town, so he was well known for his business experience.

However, Gabe had been finding problems with the mine operations and had mentioned them to Martin repeatedly, advising that the mine safety was being compromised. Martin didn't care. All he cared about was cutting corners, and Gabe suspected he was skimming off the top without letting the company know what he was doing.

Gabe's suspicions fueled Martin to make sure he tarnished Gabe's name around town so no one would ever believe him. He'd accused him of stealing, cheating, anything he could think of. And it didn't help when Gabe's own brother Davis believed it all to be true.

Davis had raised him after their parents died, and over the years, had become consumed with the need to become wealthy and respected. He didn't care who he hurt, including his brother. Davis wanted to be on the good side of Martin, believing he was the man who could help him achieve his success.

On the day he was killed, Davis had come to the mines to argue with Gabe over some rumor he'd heard about him in town. Gabe had walked away, tired of the accusations.

The mine foreman had threatened to fire him, and Davis hadn't wanted the family name to be tarnished, so had offered to fill in for Gabe that day if they didn't fire him.

Once again, trying to be the hero, without giving Gabe the benefit of the doubt.

There was an explosion in the mine that day. It killed several men, including his brother.

Gabe's name had been blacklisted

around town, so he'd left, determined never to show his face around there again. If the people of the community were more inclined to believe a man like Paine, then he'd be more than happy to turn his back and never step foot there again.

But he hadn't been able to go much farther until he knew his sister-in-law and nephew would be taken care of.

And now it looked like he just might have to show his face back in Heartsbridge again. If they all believed him to be a thief and scoundrel, well then maybe it was time to prove them right after all.

Chapter 2

*C*harlie Langley stepped off the bus, and looked around the small town. It looked like a nice place, and she hoped it was the kind of town her brother would be inclined to stay in when he arrived. The last text she'd received from him had said he was stopping in a town called Heartsbridge, Texas, then he'd probably be moving on from there.

They hadn't spoken in a while, so

she'd been happy to get his text out of the blue, but she knew she didn't even deserve to have that much communication from him. She'd treated him badly, and she wasn't sure if he could ever forgive her.

She needed to find him. Not only to make amends to the only family she had left, at least who cared about her anyway. But also to get away from the man she knew would never stop looking until he found her. And she was terrified of what he'd do when he did.

Hunger pains rumbled in her stomach, but she knew she didn't have much money left. Maybe the little diner she could see next door would have something small she could eat to fill the void.

She only had one small bag, that held a change of clothes and a few of her personal items. It was all she'd been able to grab when she'd run from Derrick, not wanting to take any more time than she needed.

The small bell above the door jingled, announcing her entrance. The diner had a homey, old-fashioned feel, and she immediately felt safe for the first time in weeks. She wasn't quite sure what it was about the place, but the atmosphere was comforting.

Taking a stool at the far end of the counter, she placed her bag on the floor by her feet. She was so tired, and what she wouldn't give for just a few minutes rest. But her hunger needed to be dealt with first. She'd figure out where to go after that.

"Hi, my name's Moira. What can I get for you?" A kind woman with red hair pulled back in a ponytail came over from behind the counter. She smiled warmly at Charlie, then squinted her eyes together briefly. "You look familiar. Do I know you?"

Charlie laughed softly. "No, I've never been here before."

"Hmm...well, my mistake. Can I

interest you in a hot beef sandwich? It's the special today, and it comes with sweet potato fries, a drink, and a piece of pie for dessert."

Charlie looked at the board behind her, and noticed the price. It was a good deal, but she knew she didn't have that much money left. Not if she hoped to afford a place to stay tonight.

"Actually, could I just have a glass of water and one of those pieces of pie? Apple, if you have it."

Moira looked at her for a moment, then tipped her head slightly. "You're sure you wouldn't like the full meal? You look like you've been traveling awhile, so I'd venture to guess you just got off the bus that pulled in a few minutes ago."

Charlie's cheeks started to burn. "I'm sure. I'm not really hungry." She smiled weakly at Moira, hoping the woman wouldn't see her shame.

Even as she said the words, the smell of the roast beef coming from the kitchen made her stomach rumble loudly.

Moira nodded, then turned to head back to the kitchen. While she waited, Charlie let her glance take in the diner around her. She wondered if Noah had stopped here on his way by. She doubted anyone would ever remember him, but maybe this Moira woman would remember a man fitting his description coming in a few weeks ago.

Lost in her thoughts, she jumped when Moira walked back over and set a plate down in front of her filled with gravy dripping over the sides of a hot beef sandwich, steam swirling from the top. A pile of crisp, orange fries filled the rest of the plate. Charlie lifted her eyes to Moira's, ready to tell her she'd made a mistake.

Moira was now pouring water from a pitcher into her glass, and smiled at her. "We had a mix-up back in the kitchen, and we thought instead of just throwing this out, we'd see if anyone could eat it. It would be a shame to see it go to waste. Of course, it's our mistake, so it will be no charge to you. No more than the pie you'd ordered." Moira reached over and grabbed a large slice of apple pie and set it beside her plate.

Charlie looked down at the steaming plate in front of her, the smell of the beef and gravy making her mouth water. "Well, thank you. I can try. I'm not sure if I can eat it all though." She knew without a doubt she could. But she felt like she should at least pretend to argue, especially since she had no doubt in her mind there wasn't really a mix-up in the kitchen.

Somehow this woman had sensed how hungry she was, and this was her way of making sure she was fed. Charlie hated feeling like she was a charity case, but she was so hungry she didn't want to turn the food down.

She suddenly felt a sob catch in her

throat, and swallowed hard, hoping to keep it from making its way to the surface. She hadn't known much kindness in a long time, and the stress of the past few days, weeks even, was catching up to her.

"How about you come and join me in the back. I have a room there where you can sit and eat in private, and maybe even have a rest."

Charlie lifted her gaze to Moira's, her eyes filled with unshed tears. All she could do was nod her head. She didn't want to break down and cause a scene in front of everyone else.

Moira took her plates and started to walk toward the kitchen, tipping her head for Charlie to follow. Grabbing her bag, she hurried to catch up. Moving in behind the counter, she followed Moira through the kitchen to a door just off the side. She kept her eyes down, not wanting anyone else to see the tears.

There was a small desk inside the

room, and a comfy looking old couch. Moira set the plates on the desk, then turned and smiled at her. "You can sit down here and enjoy your meal in some peace and quiet. I'll come back in a bit and maybe we can visit. You look like you could use a friend right now."

Charlie was still afraid to speak, knowing once she did, she'd probably open a floodgate of emotion. So she simply nodded and sat down in the chair behind the desk.

As Moira stepped out and closed the door behind her, Charlie let the tears fall. Picking up her knife and fork, she cut into the food in front of her. It had been a while since she'd had a proper meal, so she savored every bite.

And while the food started to fill her hunger, she let herself enjoy the moment of feeling safe. Because what Moira didn't realize was just how true those words "you look like you could use a friend" were.

Chapter 3

"You're welcome to stay here and rest as long as you need to." Moira had taken the dishes back to the kitchen and was now sitting on a chair across from the couch Charlie had moved to. It felt so good to just be able to relax for a few minutes.

But she knew she didn't have a lot of time. He'd find her soon. She wasn't safe yet.

He was going to make her pay for

what she'd done to him before she left, of that she had no doubt.

"Thank you so much for everything, but I really need to keep moving. I'm looking for my brother. He's the only family I have left, and the last time we saw each other he may have believed I didn't really need him in my life anymore."

Moira's eyebrows creased together. "Why would he think that?"

Charlie shrugged, not wanting to discuss her previous situation. But she sensed that Moira was someone she could confide in.

"I was with a man who wasn't what you would call a kind person. He controlled every aspect of my life. And that included who I could and couldn't see." She looked down at her hands clasped together tightly in her lap. "Including my brother, Noah."

A slight gasp made her lift her eyes back up to Moira's face. Moira was leaning forward in her chair and her eyes had widened to twice their size. "Your brother's name is Noah?" Her voice sounded slightly unsure. "That's why you look so familiar. The dark hair and eyes."

"Noah was here? You remember him?" Charlie jumped from the couch, moving to stand right in front of Moira. "Please, tell me you know where he is now."

Moira's face had suddenly turned a bright shade of red, and she swallowed as she brought her hands up to pull down on her cheeks. The woman wasn't answering, obviously trying to find a way to tell her something.

Her stomach had a sinking feeling.

"Charlie, why don't you come and sit back down over here and I'll try to see if I can help you." Moira stood and took one of her hands, leading her back to the couch.

"What is it, Moira? Is he okay?" What was the woman so afraid to tell her?

"Oh yes, he's fine, but he's not here anymore."

Charlie had a strong suspicion Moira knew more than she was saying. "Do you know where he's gone?"

Moira sat beside her on the couch, and Charlie watched her as she absently reached up and touched an old timepiece she was wearing around her neck. If Charlie wasn't so worried, and desperate for answers, she'd have asked Moira about it. There was obviously a sentimental reason for her to wear something like that.

Suddenly, Moira pulled it out farther and looked down at it with a confused expression. She lifted her eyes and looked at Charlie. "The hands are moving," her voice was barely above a whisper.

Charlie wasn't in the mood for Moira to be changing the subject to something as trivial as her old timepiece suddenly working.

"Look, Moira, I appreciate everything you've done for me. But I don't think you realize the situation completely. I need to find Noah. Do you know where I can find him or not?"

"I do. But I don't think you're going to believe me."

"I don't care if he's hopped a ship to Antarctica. If you know where he is, just tell me!" Charlie was beginning to think Moira might be a bit melodramatic.

Moira took her hand. "Noah was in here quite a few weeks ago now. He mentioned that he had a sister, and that you didn't need him anymore. He said he didn't have anyone who needed him, or any reason to be around here. So I helped him find the place he did belong."

"What are you talking about? Just tell me where he is so I can go there." Maybe this woman was a recruiter for some weird cult. No thanks. She'd just left one controlling situation. She sure wasn't going to be dumb enough to get into another one. But that didn't sound like Noah. What was going on here?

Moira was chewing on her lip as she stared at her intently. "Your brother has gone to another time." Charlie started to pull her hand away, realizing now that this woman wasn't right in the head. But Moira held it firm. "You have to let me explain this to you, and then I can get you to him. If that's what you want."

"Of course, that's what I want. Haven't I been telling you that?" My God, I hope this woman hadn't put anything strange in her food.

"Well, when your brother was here, my timepiece let me know that he needed to be in a different time with the woman his heart was supposed to be with."

Charlie sat with her mouth gaping open. "So...my brother has gone just poof, disappeared into another time." She flung her hands out dramatically. "A black hole somewhere? That's what I'm supposed to believe?"

"He's gone back in time to Heartsbridge of 1880. And whether you believe me or not is irrelevant. You will see for yourself soon enough if you decide you want to find him."

Charlie shook her head. She was obviously more tired than she'd realized. This wasn't making any sense. "Can you prove my brother was even here? I'm sorry if you're offended, but you have to realize all of this sounds just a little bit...no—a whole lot—crazy."

Moira smiled. "Trust me, I felt the exact same way." The woman stood up and walked toward a door at the back of the room. "Here, follow me."

Charlie wasn't sure she should trust her. What if she was going to be abducted and held captive or something? But something told her to see what Moira wanted to show her. When they stepped out into the back of the diner, Charlie gasped, then ran toward the truck parked there.

Noah's old beat-up truck sat in the sunlight.

"I wasn't really sure what to do with it after he left, so I had it towed around to the back."

Charlie spun to face Moira. "Why would he leave his truck behind? What have you done to him?" She was starting to feel hysterical. Something wasn't adding up with all of this.

But before she could figure it out in her mind, a familiar red Mustang drove past the end of the alley, and toward the front of the diner. Her hand flew to her mouth, muffling her cry.

"How did he find me?" she demanded of Moira.

Moira was looking around confused, then she seemed to realize something and grabbed her by the arm, pulling her back inside, and closing the door firmly behind her.

"No, I need to get away. Do you have the keys to Noah's truck? I have to get out of here." Fear gripped her, leaving her throat so dry she could barely choke the words out.

"Do you have a cell phone?" Charlie just nodded as Moira asked her the question.

"He probably put some kind of tracking on it."

Charlie closed her eyes tightly. Of course, he'd have done that. She thought she was being so careful, not using credit cards or anything that could be tracked. Meanwhile, he'd been following her the whole time.

Moira helped her to sit back down, then crouched down in front of her. "Give me your phone."

Charlie shook her head. "No, I don't want to drag you into it. This is my fight."

"Listen, I told you I'd get you to your

brother. So now you need to trust me. Give me your phone, and let me handle whoever is on the other side of that door. By the time he realizes you must have 'dropped' your phone when you passed through here, you will be gone. You'll be safe. I promise."

Something in Moira's eyes, and the sureness in her voice calmed her. She took her phone out of her bag and handed it to her.

"You can try, but I don't think he'll give up that easily."

Moira winked at her. "Well, he's not going to have much choice." She stood up and walked to the door, then stopped and looked back at her before she went through.

"Say hi to your brother for me."

With those words, she closed the door behind her. Charlie had never been so confused in her life. How was she going to say hi to her brother, when Moira still hadn't told her where to find him?

The room started to feel like it was spinning, and she tried to call out for Moira. Something wasn't right, but she couldn't stand up. Oh no. She *had* put something in the food. This is a crazy nightmare. She didn't know whether to be more afraid of Moira or her ex.

The door thumped as he banged it with his fist, and he yelled out, "I know she was here. This time I'm not going to let her get away so easily."

She dropped her head into her hands, wishing she could start fresh, and go somewhere where he'd never find her again.

That was the last thought she had as blackness overtook her.

Chapter 4

*O*pening her eyes, Charlie squinted them against the brightness of the room. Her head had fallen back against the couch, and she must have passed out. Her head was heavy and her pulse was racing as she tried to lift her head to look around.

She must have drugged me. I have to get out of here.

But something about the room seemed

different, although she couldn't quite figure it out. Everything seemed darker and dustier for some reason, and she couldn't remember seeing the old antique washstand in that corner.

She tried to swallow against the dryness of her throat, but ended up coughing and sputtering as the air from the room choked her. She tried to stand, but her legs felt weak. She decided to sit for a moment and get her strength back.

What had happened to her? She didn't think she'd ever passed out before, at least not that she could remember. Maybe she'd been drugged—she must have used a horse tranquilizer. Or a new worry filled her mind. What if she'd had a stroke?

"I'm glad to see you're awake. I've brought you a cup of water."

Charlie's eyebrows came together in confusion as she watched Moira walk back into the room. She was wearing some ridiculous dress now, and her hair was in a long braid at the back. She handed Charlie a cold metal cup filled with water.

She wondered if it was safe to take a sip but her throat was so dry she took a long swallow. Charlie brought the cup back down and looked around the room. Now that she was more awake, she realized things looked more different than she'd originally thought. The cup in her hands looked old and worn, similar to an old tin cup her grandfather had in his kitchen when she was just a child.

Who still used cups like these?

Her head lifted and she met the eyes of the woman who was standing watching her closely. She had a kind smile on her face, but for some reason she looked different.

Yes, she'd definitely been slipped something. But why?

"Moira?"

"No, my name's Cissie. Moira sent you to me."

Charlie reached up and pinched the bridge of her nose, while closing her eyes tightly. This woman was obviously as crazy as her twin.

"Listen, I'm tired, and I have no idea what is going on. Where's Derrick?" She didn't hear him banging anymore, so she assumed these women had got rid of him somehow.

Cissie's eyebrows came together. "Derrick?"

Sighing loudly, Charlie couldn't even hide her frustration. "Yes, my ex-boyfriend. The one who was pounding down the door a few minutes ago."

Cissie tilted her head. "Did Moira explain anything to you? About where you were being sent?"

"She said something about a different time where my brother is, but honestly, I think both of you are seriously one slice short of a loaf. I've tried to be patient, because I do appreciate the help Moira gave me. But I don't appreciate how it was done and right now, I just want to put my head on a pillow and sleep for about twenty-four hours straight." She stood up and went to grab her bag. Looking around the couch where she'd left it, she started to panic when she realized it was gone.

"Where did you guys put my bag?" She turned an accusing glare to Cissie. "And where did Moira go now anyway?"

This time it was Cissie who sighed loudly. "I think the easiest thing will be for you to just come with me." Cissie started to walk toward the back door that led to the alley where Noah's truck was parked.

Good, at least she might be able to take his truck and put some distance between herself and this place.

Cissie opened the door, then stepped back. Before Charlie could walk through, Cissie reached out and placed her hand on her arm. "What Moira told you was true. Is your brother's name Noah Langley by any chance?"

Charlie stopped dead in her tracks. "Yes, that's him. Do you know where he is?"

Hope once again sparked in her.

Cissie nodded. "I do. He's living about twenty miles from town. It would take a few hours to ride out to his place."

Charlie laughed. "Twenty miles isn't that far at all. We could be there a lot faster than that."

"We'd be going by horse."

Cissie took her shoulder, and gently turned her to look out the door. Charlie could see riders on horses making their way down the back streets, and a few wagons were on the other side of the alley. There wasn't a car in sight.

Her head slowly turned to the corner where her brother's truck had been parked. There was nothing there.

Her heart started to race as she looked around and finally noticed all the buildings were different. Everything looked like it was taken from an old western movie. A woman walked past the end of the alleyway, and she wore a dress similar to the one Cissie was wearing.

"What's going on?" the words came out as a whisper.

"Your brother is here. And the year is 1880. He's happy, safe, and is in fact now married to the woman he was sent here to find." Cissie pulled her back inside and closed the door behind her. She held her hand on Charlie's elbow as she led her back to the couch.

"Can you take me to Noah?" She needed to see him. He would be able to explain what was going on. He'd looked after her all the years they were growing up, and he'd always been able to fix things. He'd know what to do. If she truly had just suffered some kind of medical emergency, or been drugged... Or maybe she was just starting to lose her mind, he could take care of her.

"I know this is very difficult to believe, and I assure you when your brother arrived, he didn't want to believe it either. But what I'm saying is true, and you've been sent here for a reason. Usually it is to find your "heart match" or the person you're supposed to be with, but in your case, it could be just for the chance to make things right with your brother."

Charlie couldn't take her eyes off Cissie. Everything about her seemed genuine, and as hard as it was for her to make sense of it all, there was just something about the way she spoke that caused Charlie some hesitation. Could she be telling the truth?

She stood back up, pushing past Cissie to go to a small window at the back of the room. She peered outside, noticing the wagons and horses again. There were a few people walking behind the alley, and Charlie felt her stomach clench when she realized they were all wearing the same kind of clothes as Cissie.

If this was some kind of trick being played on her, someone had sure gone out of their way to pull it off.

But there was no one in the world who knew Charlie enough to play a prank this big on her.

Which only left one possibility.

Cissie was telling the truth.

Chapter 5

*E*verything around her was moving at a slower pace. That was something she'd noticed immediately when she'd stepped outside in the morning air. People bustled around, women went inside the building with the large Drayson's Mercantile sign above it across the street, while the men stood outside talking.

Men on horses rode past, tipping their hats down in greeting to her as they went by.

Families rode in wagons, kicking dust up behind them as they rolled by. Everyone seemed happy and friendly, giving her a sense of calmness after the events of the past few days.

Cissie had told her she'd already made plans to take supplies to some families out of town today, so she wouldn't be able to take her to Noah until tomorrow. She'd told her to just take a look around the town and get a feel for everything. They'd spent most of the evening discussing everything she needed to know for this time period so she could fit in.

However, when Charlie looked down at the extravagant gown Cissie had pulled out of the trunk for her to wear, she was quite sure she wasn't going to fit in so easily in this small, western town.

But Cissie had promised to find her something more fitting when she returned, stating this was the only dress she had that would fit Charlie for now.

Holding the small parasol over her head, she'd laughed when Cissie had handed it to her. Although at the moment with the sun beating down from the sky, she reluctantly admitted to herself that she was actually relieved to have it. Even if she did look like she'd just walked off the set for Gone with the Wind.

And the underthings Cissie had given her were all scratchy and itchy, making her feel the heat a hundred times more than her old T-shirt and capris she'd been wearing when she got here. She'd had to put those away, knowing she'd stick out like even more of a sore thumb wearing those clothes than this ridiculous get-up.

She couldn't get over the peacefulness around her without the constant sound of car engines around her though. It wasn't something she'd ever noticed, but being here she realized there wasn't any of the constant background noise usually heard in a town in the middle of the afternoon.

The sounds were different. And even though the buildings looked like they had been thrown together hastily and without much thought to how they were built, there was a certain charm that wasn't present in modern-day buildings.

Walking past the building beside Cissie's, a stagecoach sat with people waiting inside as bags were thrown up on top. People milled about on the wooden walkway, still holding bags in their hands. They'd probably just been dropped off. She smiled to herself when she realized the stagecoaches actually looked a lot like they did in movies she'd seen, but they were a bit larger than she'd imagined.

She was so lost in her thoughts, she didn't even realize she'd wandered all the way around behind the alley of the boardinghouse, up past a few more buildings and almost to the edge of the town. Heartsbridge of this time was quite a bit smaller than the one she'd come into on a large passenger bus.

Turning to go back in the other direction, she stopped when she heard hooves pounding the ground behind her. Before she could look back to see if she was in the way, she was grabbed around the waist and dragged up over the back of the horse, and thrown onto her stomach over someone's legs.

She tried to scream, but a hand went over her mouth, holding her firm.

Like a scene out of every western movie her grandfather had made her watch, she realized she was being abducted by some outlaw in the old west. Somehow though, she knew this person was not going to be any Clint Eastwood.

If she hadn't believed she was losing her mind before, she was sure this would be what pushed her over the edge.

***

She fell to the ground with a thud, landing unceremoniously on her backside as her legs buckled beneath her. Pushing back with her legs, she tried to get herself away far enough to stand up and make a run for it. Even as she thought about it, she knew it would be futile to try outrunning horses, but she had to at least try.

She hadn't spent weeks planning an escape and running from one man intent on hurting her only to be thrown into the exact same situation now.

Before she could stand, though, the man who'd abducted her grabbed her arm and pulled her to her feet. Her heart was pounding with fear, but she wasn't going to let him see how scared she was. As she was dragged in front of the horse, she realized there were more horses there, and another man stood in front of them.

If not for the terrifying situation she was in, she might have been able to let herself admit the man she was now looking at was exactly how she'd always imagined the rugged, tough cowboy in the old west to be.

Except this wasn't a movie, and this man wasn't a cowboy. He was obviously some kind of heathen and she had no doubt he was dangerous. A gentleman wouldn't be involved in kidnapping a woman off the street in the middle of the day.

As her eyes looked at the new man in front of her, her hands were pulled together and tied in front of her by the man who'd grabbed her.

"Are you sure you got the right woman?" The man, who wasn't a cowboy, walked toward them, eyeing her up and down. "Although, by the looks of her, I'd say she's exactly the type of woman he'd have ordered."

What were they talking about?

"I'm not sure who you think you have, but I assure you, you have the wrong woman," her voice shook with fear as she tried to make herself sound more sure.

The man lifted an eyebrow and grinned. "Well, if you don't know who I think you are, then how do you know I have the wrong woman?"

The other man pushed her to the side by the new horses. Both men looked at her for a moment before turning back to each other to talk, obviously not worried about her getting away. "She was wandering the streets near the stagecoach station. And there aren't many women around Heartsbridge wearing fancy clothes like that. She has to have come from the city."

"Hakan, you mean you didn't even ask her who she was before you grabbed her?"

She was finally able to get a good look at the man who'd pulled her off the street, and she realized with a gasp he was a Native American. Except, back in this time period, from everything she'd read in books, they weren't likely to be friendly to a white woman.

Hakan just shrugged. "Didn't need to

ask. If she's not the right woman, I'll just get rid of her and go back to get the one you can get the money for."

Her heart leaped into her throat. *What did he mean by "get rid of her?"* Obviously, they believed she was someone they could ransom for her return.

At that moment, she realized her best bet to get out of this alive was to pretend she was whoever they thought she was. At least until she could make her escape.

The other man walked toward her. He brought his face closer, looking at her intently. "What's your name?"

She swallowed hard, not wanting to answer. She didn't know what name they were looking for.

While she hesitated, Hakan walked up and looked at her too. "What does it matter? Not like you knew what her name was going to be, Gabe. You just told me she was coming in on a stagecoach in the next few days to marry that man you hate. You said she'd be dressed like a lady, coming from the city. I didn't think I needed to sit down and discuss the details with her."

The man called Gabe clenched his eyes tight for a moment and sighed. "No, Hakan, you're right. But I just assumed you'd at least make sure you had the right woman before throwing her on your horse and racing out of town. You're sure no one saw you?"

Hakan laughed. "Do you even need to ask?" He moved to hop back onto the horse he'd used to abduct her. "Now we are paid up." With that, he kicked his heels into his horse and turned to race away.

She was left shaking as she stood in front of the man with the cowboy hat. He looked angry and frustrated as he turned back to face her.

"What's your name? And can you tell me what you were doing in Heartsbridge?"

She knew now that he didn't know the name, but she also knew what she needed to pretend to keep herself alive.

"My name is Charlotte. And I was there to meet the man I am to marry."

If it would buy her some time, she'd pretend to be the Queen of England if she had to.

Chapter 6

"I'm sorry you've been caught in the middle of a dispute I'm having with your intended groom, however it's time Martin Paine had to pay for some of the wrongs he's done to others around here. And if I know him as well as I think I do, he won't take kindly to knowing I've got something of his he's already invested heavily in." He looked at the woman who was staring at him like he'd grown horns. Which he figured in her mind, he likely had.

"I assume Martin paid for your ticket

to get to Heartsbridge? From what I heard, you came from Boston, so I'm sure it would've cost a pretty penny."

She scrunched her eyes together and shook her head at him. "So, you believe this man, Martin, is going to pay you a ransom for me? And then what? You'll just let me go?"

His heart did a strange clench as he heard the fear in her voice, mixed with the hope that he would let her go once he got his money. Guilt tore at his insides, but he couldn't back down now.

"I promise you, I'm not going to harm you. Unfortunately, you're just a necessary means for me to make him pay what I'm owed. And if I can offer some advice to you, I'd suggest that when I do let you go, you hop on the first horse out of town as fast as you can. A man like Martin Paine isn't one who would treat a lady kindly."

He walked over and took hold of the scratchy rope binding her hands together and pulled, trying not to look into the dark brown eyes staring at him with terror. He'd always known he wasn't a good man, but now seeing how low he'd sunk reflected in her gaze, he had to swallow the bitterness he felt.

"Where are you taking me?"

He brought her over to the horses, and turned back to face her. "Can you ride?"

Suddenly, she stopped walking, making the rope burn his hand where it slid from his grip. He turned back to face her, his eyes wrinkling together in confusion. He noticed wetness in the eyes glaring back at him.

"I asked you where you're taking me? I know I'm just a pawn in your stupid game with this man, but I deserve an answer. I'm tired, I've been through more than my fair share of mistreatment at the hands of a man in the past few months, and right now all I want is an honest answer."

He stared at her, stunned by the sudden fire he could see lighting behind her gaze.

She was terrified, but she was also not willing to just go quietly without a fight. This wasn't a woman who deserved to be stuck with a man like Martin for the rest of her life. Maybe someday she could see that he'd actually done her a favor by saving her from that fate.

"I've got a place just outside of Maplesville where I've been staying. We'll stay there until I can let your future groom know what my terms are."

"And aren't you afraid the law is going to be coming after you?"

He laughed. "Well, that's the thing. My friend Hakan is good at moving around without being noticed. I have no doubt he got out of town without anyone seeing him. And as far as Martin is concerned, he'll probably just assume you're taking longer to get here, or maybe he'll even think you ran off with his money. So by the time I have a chance to let him know what really happened, we'll be well hidden."

She looked up at the horses. "And you expect me to ride on this horse, with this ridiculous dress on and my hands still tied in front of me?"

He was shocked to hear a woman admit her dress was ridiculous. Why would she wear it if she didn't like it? But even as he stood wondering about that, he admitted to himself he might not have thought everything through, especially when he saw the amount of fabric she did have on her dress. He wasn't sure how she'd even stay sitting in the saddle.

"You could ride in front of me."

She rolled her eyes. "No, thank you. I'll take my chances of falling and possibly cracking my skull on a rock. I'm perfectly capable of riding astride without anyone needing to hold on to me." His mouth fell open as she strode over to put her booted foot into the stirrup, and reached up with her bound hands to grab the horn of the saddle.

What was it about the way she spoke that sounded so different? It must be the way they talked in Boston, because he'd never heard a woman talk like her before. And he realized the fear she'd been feeling when she first arrived had somehow now turned into what he almost believed to be annoyance.

Everything about this plan wasn't working quite as he'd hoped, and now he wished he'd just left things well enough alone. Originally he'd planned to just sweep the woman off her feet and steal her from Martin that way, but then he'd realized he'd be stuck with her—and he wasn't the type of man to marry some uppity woman from the city.

So Hakan had offered to grab her for him. The man felt he owed a debt to Gabe from the time he'd saved his son from drowning in a river over by Maplesville.

And since Gabe didn't have any other

ideas, he figured it was as good a plan as any. Everyone thought he was a thief, so why not steal a woman right from under Martin's nose?

He continued to watch the woman, finding himself smiling at her determination to get up on that horse by herself, even with her tied hands and mountains of skirts. She had managed to pull herself up slightly a couple of times, but had to step back down each time her leg tangled in her skirts.

"You know, there does tend to be a lot of wolves out around these parts once the sun goes down. I'd prefer to be in the safety of the cabin by then."

She swung around and glared at him, her hands still up on the saddle, and her one leg up in the stirrup. He was doing his best to keep his eyes averted, but he could see some skin peeking out from under the skirt.

"You're just trying to scare me." He could hear the shakiness in her voice as she tried to pretend she wasn't really worried about the mention of wolves.

He shrugged and walked over beside her. "Have you ever seen what a hungry wolf can do to a person?"

Her eyes grew even larger, which he'd been sure wouldn't have been possible. He'd noticed her eyes immediately, and had to admit there was something in those hazel depths that seemed to keep drawing his eyes back.

He saw her swallow. "Well, if you just give me a hand, that would be fine. *But watch where you put them.*" She ground the last part out between clenched teeth. He felt bad scaring her again, but the truth was, he just needed to get home and figure out what he was going to do with her. He ignored the nagging voice that kept telling him to take her back to Heartsbridge. The other voice was telling him he still needed her to make Martin pay.

Placing his hands around her waist, he hoisted her up into the saddle. She almost slid right off to the other side as her boot got caught up again in the fabric. If he didn't know better, he was sure he heard her curse under her breath as she tried to get herself sitting properly.

But he was sure he'd never heard a woman use that word before, and certainly not one as refined as her, that would be coming from Boston.

"This dress is awful. How do women ride with these things on?"

His eyes widened as he watched her pull the skirt of her dress right up, exposing her small boots and the full extent of her lower leg.

For a woman who was supposed to have been brought up properly, she sure was acting different from what he'd expected.

"You know, it isn't proper for a lady to be showing as much skin as you are." As soon as the words left his mouth, he clenched his lips back together. Why would he try to make her cover up, when what he was seeing was so enjoyable to look at?

"Well, I'm not a lady. And in case you forgot, these aren't exactly normal circumstances. So, can we just get moving before those wolves you mentioned show up?"

Even though she was putting on a tough exterior, he could see she was genuinely worried about being out here at the mercy of the wild animals.

Hopping up on his own horse to start leading them toward home, the thought popped into his head that the poor woman would probably be safer with the wolves than with Martin.

Yes, he was definitely doing her a favor.

Chapter 7

"Can't you at least untie my hands? It's not like I can get away when my horse is tied to yours." Her wrists were starting to hurt where the rope was scratching against her skin. It was so hot outside, she was sure she was about to pass out from the heat building up and being held under this cumbersome outfit. And to top it off, now she desperately needed to use a bathroom, but she knew there would be no rest stops with nice clean toilets for her along the way.

She was going to have to somehow hoist this dress up and squat on the side of the dirt road they were traveling on. Of course, she was going to have to somehow let him know she needed to stop first. At the moment he was riding ahead and not even responding to her at all.

"Okay, listen. I really don't know any other way to say it, so I'm just going to let you know the truth. I need to pee."

Her horse walked straight into the back end of his as he stopped suddenly and whipped his head around.

"What did you just say?"

The look on his face almost made up for the discomfort she was feeling.

She shrugged. "I said, I need to pee. I need to get off this horse, head into a bush somewhere and squat on the ground to pee. And do all of this while trying to keep this abomination of a dress from getting in it."

His mouth hung open as his dark brown eyes held hers. He wasn't moving a muscle, just staring at her in shock. She didn't care. Cissie had told her she needed to use the mannerisms and expressions expected of a woman back in this century so no one would start to wonder about where she came from. But she figured these circumstances were far removed from anything Cissie expected her to be living.

Quite frankly, she didn't care one bit what the man thought of her at this point. Let him wonder.

He cleared his throat and shook his head quickly, before throwing his leg over and dismounting from his horse. As he walked back to her, his eyebrows were furrowed together.

"A simple mention that you needed to stop to take care of business would have been sufficient."

He reached his hand up and she tried to take it, but the rope still held her own hands tightly together. She couldn't hold on enough to feel safe to dismount. Before she had a chance to figure out what to do, he reached up and grabbed her around the waist, pulling her down to the ground.

Her legs were unsteady and she fell into the front of him. She came up against the hardness of his chest as he put his hands on her arms to help her stand upright.

Pushing herself back quickly, she shook to try and get her dress to fall back down around her ankles. Everything was bunched up beneath her, and even though she'd kill to have a pair of shorts to wear, she wasn't about to let this man see her legs under the dress at this moment.

"Can you untie my hands? Or will you be coming with me to assist?" She didn't know why she was standing here goading him into an argument when she really was starting to feel desperate for the shelter of the bush.

She was almost sure she noticed his

cheeks go a shade darker above the unshaven stubble of his jawline. And his teeth were ground together as he reached for her. "I'll cut the rope, but just remember what can happen to a woman on her own out there. You'd make a good meal for the wolves that have likely been trailing us the whole way." He reached into a pocket on his saddle and pulled out a knife.

Her heart pounded as he came closer and flicked the wicked looking blade open to cut the rope. She swallowed against the dryness of her throat as she realized how easily he could have used that blade to hurt her if he'd wanted to.

But she wasn't going to let him see her fear. She turned and quickly made her way behind the small bush that would act as shelter from his prying eyes. One thing she had already decided she hated about this time period was the lack of suitable bathroom facilities.

At Cissie's she'd had to walk to a

"privy" as the woman had called it out behind the building. Overnight, she'd then pointed out a small china pot Charlie was expected to use if she needed to go. And now she was about to crouch down on the ground while holding miles of skirts up around her waist.

To make things worse, if that was even possible, all she could think about were the wolves the man kept mentioning. Her eyes scanned the area warily to see if any eyes were watching her back.

She hurried as fast as her dress would allow, then stood, quickly pulling everything back down as she stepped away. She had a moment of indecision as she realized she could make a run for it and try to get away from him.

Common sense prevailed though as she also realized she didn't have a clue where they were, or how to even get back to Heartsbridge. Of course, the threat of wild animals feasting on her didn't sound too appealing either.

"Glad you didn't need my help. The amount of grumbling I could hear coming from behind that bush, I was sure you were in a dire situation and I'd have to come to your rescue."

Her eyebrow went up as she glared at him. "Rescue me? When you're the one I need rescuing from? In case you've forgotten, you abducted me just a few short hours ago."

"Minor detail. And besides, it wasn't technically me who abducted you. I've just been left to figure out what to do with you."

This time it was her mouth hanging open. "If you didn't want to abduct me, why don't you just let me go?"

He shrugged as he came over and put his hand on her elbow, pulling her back toward her horse. "Maybe I'm just enjoying the pleasant company."

"You're insane." She truly didn't have

any other words at the moment.

"You're not the first to tell me that." This time he shot her a dazzling smile, that under any other circumstances she was sure would have her weak in the knees. He really was a handsome man—for a criminal. And she'd been attracted to too many of those kinds of men in her lifetime. She knew what they were like under that good-looking exterior.

His hands moved toward her waist, so she brushed them away. "I'm perfectly capable of getting on my horse by myself now that I have the use of both hands, thank you."

The smile on his face seemed to turn into more of a smirk as he nodded and took a step back. "By all means, my lady. Don't let me get in your way."

She'd grown up around horses on her grandfather's farm, spending many hours in the saddle. And now she had the feeling her ability was being challenged by this outlaw.

She wasn't sure why it bothered her so much, but she intended to prove to him she was more than capable.

Hiking her skirt up to her thighs, she enjoyed the shocked look on his face as she shot him a smug look. Her foot pushed into the stirrup, and still holding the dress around her waist, she threw her other leg up and over the back of the horse, holding the horn of the saddle with her other hand.

She made a show of placing her skirt at a more respectable length around her legs, patting the fabric down and over her ankles.

"Are you just going to stand there gawking, or could we get going? As you've so kindly pointed out, I'd just as soon not sit here waiting to be eaten by wolves."

Chapter 8

*H*e couldn't figure out what to think about this woman. But he did know for a fact that after spending the past few hours with her, Martin would have been no match for her.

She'd been afraid when he first saw her being carried in draped over Hakan's legs. However, he had no doubt anyone would be afraid after being grabbed off a street by a stranger and hauled away. It had to be terrifying for a woman.

But as the day had worn on, and they'd made their way toward his cabin hidden back in the woods, she'd become increasingly less afraid. By the time they arrived, she was downright angry with him.

Perhaps he needed to remind her who was in charge. Of course, he really didn't know if he was or not, but he didn't plan to let her know that.

He'd come outside to rub down the horses, reminding her once more about the wild animals in the darkness if she tried to make her escape. That was the only time he still saw any fear in her eyes, so he knew it would be enough to keep her there until he could figure out exactly what he was going to do.

He appreciated Hakan's help, but he really did wish he'd had more time to come up with his plan.

As he walked back to the small cabin,

he noticed the sky lighting up with a storm headed their way. The first raindrop hit his cheek as he made his way onto the porch, and he removed his hat to shake the dust off as he walked through the door.

His breath caught in his throat when he came through and saw her standing there wearing one of his button up shirts, with sleeves rolled up to fit on her arms. It was tucked into a pair of his pants, hanging from her hips and held up by a piece of rope tied tightly around the waist.

She stood looking out the far window at the lightning in the sky. Her hair was pulled back and hung in a loose braid down her back. She turned to face him as she heard him come in, and crossed her arms in front of her as though to offer herself some kind of protection.

He had that familiar pang of guilt knowing she felt she'd need protecting from him.

"Mind telling me why you're wearing

my clothes?" He'd never seen a woman wearing a man's clothes in his life, especially not his. He couldn't quite understand the strange tug he could feel in his stomach. It seemed like something so intimate to be sharing clothing that had touched his skin, and were now touching hers.

"I couldn't spend another minute in that dress. The underthings were too tight and hot, and I couldn't get comfortable no matter what I did. So I figured I'd look around and find something more to my liking."

Most women would kill to have a dress as stunning as the one she'd been wearing, yet all day she'd mentioned how much she didn't like it.

He could only imagine the upbringing she must have enjoyed to be able to dispose of a fancy dress so easily, and complain about its comfort.

"Men's clothes are more to your

liking?"

She shrugged and moved to sit down on the rickety chair by the fireplace. "There's a lot about me you'll never know."

She kept her eyes facing the window, not even looking his way. He pushed his hands through his hair, wishing he could go back to this morning and not follow through with stealing this woman. It wasn't fair that she was being used to pay a debt from a man she hadn't even met.

Maybe all those years his brother had been right about him. He'd always told him he was a troublemaker. And Davis had been one of the first ones to believe the worst of him when accusations started to come from the trouble at the mines.

What he'd done today had proven his brother's opinion of him wasn't so wrong after all.

"Are you hungry?"

He realized he hadn't even offered her

anything to eat or drink all day. She was likely starving.

She laughed. "What does it matter to you? You're just another man who thinks you can treat people however you want, then come in and act nice like nothing has happened."

"Listen, I'm not happy about what I've done either. Unfortunately, your future groom left me without many choices. But I give you my word that as soon as I figure out how to make him pay up what I'm owed, you'll be set free. And while you're here, you're in no danger from me."

She slowly turned her head toward him. A flash of lightning filled the window, illuminating her against the darkening of the room. Her eyes looked hollow, as though she wasn't really seeing him. "Your *word*? I'm afraid *your word* doesn't mean much, considering you've stolen a woman off the street and dragged her out here without so much as a drink of water all day. Since you're nothing more than a criminal—and excuse me, I believe it's called outlaw back here—I don't really take much relief in *your word* that I'm in no danger with you."

He cringed at her words. What did she mean by back here? Is that what they called the more unsettled parts of the country in the east?

"You're right. I have done something for which I'm not proud of, but there's nothing I can do about that now. I don't expect you to believe my word after what you've been through today. You'll just have to judge me by what you see while you're here. Although I suspect that like most people you'll judge based on what you already have made up in your mind."

He didn't know why he suddenly felt angry. It wasn't like everything she was saying wasn't true.

But for some reason, he suddenly had the urge to prove her wrong. To prove to her that he wasn't the outlaw she believed him to be.

But how could he do that, when even he wasn't sure what was true anymore?

Chapter 9

She pulled the worn and dusty blanket up around her shoulders. It wasn't really cold in the room, but it gave her a small sense of security. Her abductor slept on the floor in the other room, just a few feet away. Outside the storm still raged on, every crack of thunder made her heart jump.

At least she wasn't hungry now. Gabe had made bacon and beans, a meal that turned out surprisingly well. Although she figured anything would have tasted good when she was that hungry.

Then there was the water he'd gotten from a pump outside—it was delicious. She'd always assumed water was just water, and she was one who always bought the bottled water which was supposed to be cleaner.

But she had to admit, this water straight from the pump, completely unfiltered, had a taste that was unlike any other water she'd ever had. Or maybe it was just because she was deliriously close to being dehydrated that made it taste so heavenly.

She rolled onto her back, staring at the ceiling. Her life had changed so much in the past few days. All she wanted was to find her brother, and somehow she'd ended up living through a scene from *Back to the Future*. She still couldn't even believe it had happened.

However, after having to use the run

down old outhouse behind the cabin earlier, with nothing more than an old newspaper to tend to her needs, she had no doubts of where she was. She shuddered as she remembered the experience.

She knew she could probably get out the window and to one of the horses, but with the storm, the wolves that she'd been warned about repeatedly, and the fact she'd be lost in the dark, she knew there wasn't any point in trying tonight.

As she lay here in the darkness, she could hear them howling outside. They sounded like they were right outside her window.

She made the decision that of the two choices, Gabe seemed to be less of a threat. He did seem to regret having done what he did, but she also knew that men like him could put on a good act of pretending they weren't as bad as you thought.

She'd spent enough time with one just like that to know she needed to keep her guard up around this man. He acted like he meant her no harm, but she had no doubt what he was capable of if she wasn't careful.

She wasn't sure why she hadn't told him the truth about who she was. In her mind she kept hearing the other man saying he'd just get rid of her, and even though he wasn't here now, she still felt uneasy. Gabe would be furious when he realized she wasn't even the right woman, and she wasn't about to find out how he'd react.

Suddenly, a loud banging noise came from outside, followed by the whinnying of the horses in the pen by the barn. She sat bolt upright, recognizing the sound of horses in distress.

Throwing her cover back, she moved to the window to see if she could see anything. The moon gave off some light, and with another flash of lightning, she could see something moving in the pen, upsetting the horses.

"Gabe, there's something in the pen

outside." She ran out to the other room, just in time to catch him already throwing his shirt on and racing to the door. He reached out and grabbed a gun from the shelf beside it.

"Stay here."

With those words, he tore out into the darkness, leaving her alone to listen to the commotion getting louder outside.

A shot rang out, sending her heart into her throat.

What if something happened to Gabe, and she was left out here alone? She didn't even know where to go, and even if she did, would she be brave enough to try?

She came from a world where she could drive in her car and know she was safe, with a GPS on her phone telling her where the next town was. Out here, she had no idea where the next house or any civilization might be.

If there was someone, or something,

out there that was even more of a threat to her than Gabe, she could now be at their mercy.

She wasn't about to sit here and wait to see what was going on. Grabbing the duster she saw by the door, she threw it over her shoulders as she ran out into the darkness. Thankfully, the storm had passed, leaving the sky clear, so she was able to make out the figures of the horses moving around in the pen giving her an idea of where to run.

She couldn't see any sign of Gabe. Even though she knew if she called out, and someone else was out here she would be putting herself in danger, she had to find out where he was. "Gabe, where are you? What's going on?"

She heard a groan. "Woman, I told you to stay inside. There are wolves out here, and obviously they're hungry. I don't need to be worrying about you too."

She moved toward the sound of his

voice, and gasped when she saw him leaning on the ground over a foal that was lying in front of him with a gash in its hind leg. The mother stood over top, her sides heaving with each breath she took.

"Oh no. What happened?"

She crouched down across from him by the foal. The poor thing was terrified, her eyes large in their sockets as she whinnied pitifully.

"The wolves have been getting bad around here lately. Must not be enough food around for them, so they've been coming onto people's properties. They try to wound their prey and then come back for them. Since the horses were penned up, they had nowhere to run." He swore under his breath, but she could still make out what he said.

"I should've put them inside the barn."

He pushed his hands under the foal, and stood, lifting it in his arms. She knew how heavy the animal had to be, but he seemed to be working on pure adrenaline.

The mare nudged him, not sure what he was doing. "It's all right, Princess, I'm just going to take her inside where it's safe."

He released the gate, and Princess followed her baby and him.

She stood and followed. "Do you have any bandages we can use to wrap the wound?" Over the years on her grandfather's farm, she'd seen many horses get tangled in barbed wire, ending up with large cuts on their legs. He'd shown her how to tend to the injuries and make sure infection didn't set in.

"No, I'll just wash it out and let it heal on its own." He stepped inside the barn, moving to place the injured foal on some straw in the corner. It wasn't a big building, and it looked like it was about to fall down around them, but at least it was some shelter from the predators that would be coming back to look for it.

"You need to wrap it up and stop the

bleeding. It will heal faster."

He glared at her, and she was shocked to see the worry and concern in his eyes over the hurt animal.

"And what makes you an expert?"

"I'm not, but I've spent enough time around horses to know how to tend to a wound like that." She turned and raced back to the house, wanting to find something clean she could use as bandages for the injured leg.

When she got back to the barn, she stopped short just inside the door as she watched the man who'd abducted her gently washing the gash with a cloth and water from a bucket. He softly whispered reassuring words to both mama and baby.

The only other man she'd ever seen be so caring with an animal was her brother Noah.

Gabe really didn't fit the criminal profile in this moment.

She cleared her throat and walked over to him. She thrust her dress at him. "Here, you can rip some of the fabric off here to use. Just wrap the wound tightly and it will help to slow the bleeding down and keep any dirt from getting in. You don't want to end up with infection."

He looked at the dress then wrinkled his eyebrows as his eyes moved to hers. "You want me to rip your fancy dress up to wrap a cut on a horse's leg?"

"Well, I looked around and didn't see a whole lot of other options that would be clean and suitable."

She started to feel uncomfortable under his stare.

Finally, he nodded and took the dress from her. He ripped a piece off the bottom with a loud tearing sound, then started to wrap it around the foal's wound. The small horse was whinnying and trying to stand up.

"It's okay, Mollie. Just let me get your

wound fixed up and you'll be running around in no time."

As she watched him work with his head down, moving his hands to quickly tie off the bleeding, she somehow sensed there was a lot more to this man than what she'd first thought.

One thing she'd learned from her grandpa was that any man who treats an animal kindly can't be a bad person.

So something didn't seem to add up with Gabe. And for some reason, she realized she wanted to find out exactly what that was.

Chapter 10

"I'm afraid there isn't much left to your dress, Charlotte."

He set the remaining fabric on the table as he came through the door. He'd stayed out in the barn with the foal last night, keeping an eye on it and changing the bandages as needed.

By this morning, Mollie was back up, limping around the stall, so he hoped she'd make a full recovery. If he could keep the wound from getting infected, she had a good chance.

He was actually surprised to find Charlotte still here. If it had been him in her position, he'd have been long gone by morning. However, he was sure the fear of the wolves had kept her from even trying to escape.

"Just call me Charlie. No one calls me Charlotte."

She was standing by the window staring out when he'd come through the door, turning to face him when he spoke. This morning, her hair was still in the braid, but pieces of it had come loose around the top from where she'd slept on it. He'd noticed she was a beautiful woman yesterday, but for some reason this morning, he could see just how much.

"Charlie? That's a man's name. It doesn't really suit you."

She sighed and rolled her eyes, then

looked back out the window. "Right, I forgot where I was. Just call me whatever you want."

Guilt washed over him again. She was obviously still upset, even after he'd promised to take her safely back home.

Clearing his throat, he moved over to the basin to wash his hands. "If you can just give me a couple more days to make sure the wolf doesn't come back for Mollie, and to keep an eye on her leg, I'll take you home. Until then, you're welcome to have free run of the place. I'll stay in the barn."

Silence filled the room as he waited for her to reply. Drying his hands, he turned to face her again. She still looked out the window, not even paying him any attention.

"Did you hear what I said?"

She finally turned and shrugged. "That's fine. I'm not really even sure where home is anyway."

He wondered if she was having

second thoughts about marrying Martin. She likely had her doubts now after hearing what kind of a man he was.

But before he could question her, she seemed to shake off her melancholy and went to sit at the table. "How's Mollie this morning?"

He went to the old stove and bent down to stoke the fire so he could at least prepare them something to eat. She didn't seem like the type of woman who'd had to cook her own meals, so he figured it would be his responsibility to make sure she was fed.

"She's good. I think she'll be all right, but it spooked all the horses pretty bad. I'm going to have to keep a close eye on things tonight to make sure the wolves know they can't get a free meal here."

He faced her as he stood back up. "How do you know so much about horses anyway? I wouldn't imagine women from the city spent a great deal of time around any animals."

"You don't know me, or how I spent my time growing up."

"You're right, Charlotte. I was just going to offer my thanks for helping me with Mollie." Obviously, she wasn't in the mood for small talk today.

She sighed, and he let his eyes move back to her. She sat with her head in her hands on the table. "I'm sorry. But you have to realize these past few days have been a bit draining. And you have kidnapped me after all. It's not like I feel like we should be sitting down and having polite conversation over breakfast."

He nodded. "Well, we have to eat. Whether or not our conversation is polite is entirely up to you."

He turned back to the stove, cracking some eggs he had in a basket on the floor into the pan that was now sizzling. He scooped some coffee grounds into the pot and set it on the back.

"Why do you hate Martin Paine so much?"

Her voice shocked him, making him drop the pot down harder on the stove than he'd thought. The banging metal on the cast iron oven surface was loud in the room.

He stepped back and spun around to face her. "I thought we weren't going to have polite conversation?"

She shrugged and kept her eyes firmly on his. "Well, I just thought I deserved to know what your problem is with the man. I mean, there must be some story if you were willing to kidnap an innocent woman over it."

He cringed at her words.

"I assure you, I've regretted that decision ever since. But there's not much I can do about it now."

"Did he steal a woman from you? Or is it just about money? I get the impression you aren't the kind of man who normally takes part in criminal activities, so he must have pushed you into it. So, what did he do?"

He stared at her in shock. The woman had a way with just speaking her mind, he had to give her that. He'd never heard a woman speak so openly. Most women tried to be coy and act like they weren't interested in anything besides what would get the man to notice them.

But Charlotte was different. He just couldn't quite figure her out.

"Well, Martin was the man hired to manage the mines just outside of Heartsbridge. I was working there, and had a few concerns about some safety issues I felt were being ignored. When I brought them to his attention, he just laughed and told me to do my job and not question the men in charge."

His heart started to race again as the familiar feeling of anger rose to the surface.

"I kept pushing, because I knew the company who owns the mine likely didn't know how badly Martin was cutting corners. But I had no way to prove it, no matter how hard I tried. My brother Davis thought the sun rose and set with Martin Paine. He wanted to have the wealth and prestige Martin did, owning land and businesses around town. He wouldn't believe anything bad about the man."

Gabe turned to give the eggs a final stir, then scraped them onto two plates. He set them on the table and grabbed the coffee pot, pouring them each a cup.

He sat down and looked across at her. She was still listening intently, her eyes on his.

"Martin started spreading stories around town that I was stealing from the mine, and showing up late for work, anything he could think of. I'd been a bit rough around the edges growing up, so the it was easy for the townsfolk to believe him."

He clenched his jaw tight. "My brother did too."

"I'm sorry. Family is supposed to always have your back." She gave him a sad smile.

"That's what I thought. My brother raised me, and I know I wasn't always easy, but I wouldn't steal or do the things I was being accused of." He nodded at her raised eyebrow when he mentioned he wouldn't steal. "Okay, until now."

"I found some papers that showed what the company had been sending Martin to pay for new safety measures, and when I confronted him, he went crazy. I knew the materials he was using wouldn't have cost that much, so I threatened to get in touch with the company. The next day, Davis came to the mine to talk to me about not causing so much trouble for Martin. I was furious, so I stormed away. The foreman at the mine said he'd fire me, and Davis had to step in and be a hero to save my job. He went in to work in my place, figuring I'd come back once I'd cooled down."

He swallowed and moved his eyes past her to the window. "There was an explosion, killing Davis and a couple other men from the mine."

The words came out through the rawness in his throat, sounding strained.

"Thanks to me, my brother was gone, leaving behind a new wife and baby. And everyone in town knew what had happened. I never went back."

"Surely you don't blame yourself for an accident?" Her eyebrows were pushed together in confusion.

"I do. But, I also don't believe it was an accident. I've just never been able to prove it."

She sharply inhaled. "You think Martin had something to do with it?"

"I know he did. And that's what made it even harder for me to swallow when I was going in every month after to pay off the farm my brother left behind. You see, it was Martin's land, but Davis had worked out an agreement to have it paid off after five years and it would be his. He only had a few more payments, so I had to make it right for his widow and my nephew. Only, after I'd paid it all off, I found out he was still expecting payment from her, and threatening to take it. He'd pocketed my money."

"Wow. I don't even know what to say. Seriously, where I come from, he'd be locked up in jail for years for doing what he did. There has to be some kind of paper trail."

He was about to take a sip from his coffee, but pulled his cup back down. "I'm not sure what you mean."

She wasn't making sense again. And what did wow mean? Had she meant to say whoa? It must be the Boston accent. It was mighty confusing at times.

"He must have some records, or some

receipts—something that would prove what he's done."

His eyebrow went up. "This is your future husband we are talking about, remember?"

She averted her eyes quickly, and started to chew on the inside of her lip. "Well, I guess since we are sharing the truth, I should tell you something too. I'm not Martin Paine's fiancée. My name's Charlie Langley. I came to Heartsbridge to find my brother, Noah."

Gabe dropped his fork. Noah Langley.

The man who was now married to his brother's widow.

His head fell into his hands as he realized the full extent of what he'd done. Not only had he committed the crime of kidnapping a woman, he'd gotten the wrong one.

Chapter 11

She sat on the edge of the pen, laughing as Mollie ran over, prancing around, hoping she'd play with her. Charlie had always loved horses, and had sorely missed them all the years she'd been living away from them.

"Looks like her leg is going to be just fine. She bounced back quickly." She looked across at Gabe who was busy working on setting a post into the ground on the other side of the pen. He'd been working at fixing up the pens for the past two days, only coming into the house to eat and wash up, saying he wanted to make sure everything was more secure for the animals.

But she also thought he was avoiding being around her too. Considering she was the one being held captive, the irony wasn't lost on her. Ever since she'd told him the truth about who she was, he'd been staying away from her.

He'd been angry at first, then had shook his head and stood to leave the kitchen, making a comment that now he was going to have to answer to her brother and would likely have to do right by her.

Whatever that was supposed to mean.

She hated to admit it, but she'd actually felt safer and more content here in the past few days than she had in a very long time.

It was so strange, considering she'd been thrown back to a different time, and then kidnapped on top of that. But considering what she'd been living with until then, she really couldn't be surprised. Sadly, this was a lot better than what she had come from.

She spent the days helping to do what she could for the pens, and just tending to the animals. She would love to walk a bit into the quiet of the brush around them and take in the beauty of this still untouched land, but she was still wary of the wild animals she knew were lying in wait just outside the property.

"I realize you're upset that you've kidnapped the wrong woman. However, you really don't need to make things worse by acting like a child who didn't get his way. The only person who has any right to be angry at the moment is me—the woman who was dragged out here to the middle of nowhere completely at the mercy of men who could do anything to her. And yet, here I am trying to make my captor talk to me." She reached out to pet Mollie's nose as she pushed up against her again.

"Seriously, I've always heard of the Stockholm Syndrome. That must be what this is. I've started to relate to my kidnapper. I'm so desperate for company I'll take whatever I can get," she spoke the words quietly for Mollie's ears only.

"What are you talking about now? Honestly, Charlotte, the things that come out of your mouth sometimes makes me truly wonder where exactly you came from. Which, I guess since you aren't coming here to marry Martin, you haven't come from Boston. So, do you want to tell me where you came from? I don't ever remember hearing how you or your brother all of a sudden ended up in Heartsbridge."

He had stopped working, and was now leaning against a post, one booted foot resting on the bottom rail as his dark eyes bore into hers.

She laughed. "You wouldn't even believe me if I told you." She could just imagine his reaction if she did.

The warmth of the sun beat down on them in the pen, while the horses grazed around them. Mollie was still coming over for attention, and Charlie realized she'd become quite fond of the little foal. Even after what it had been through, it still seemed so willing to trust.

"Try me. We are stuck together for at least another day before I can take you to your brother, which I am not looking forward to seeing his reaction, by the way. So we may as well pass the time getting to know each other."

She wasn't sure why he'd want to bother getting to know her better, but she figured it didn't really matter. It's not like she'd see him again. And she was sure she wouldn't be staying in this time. Once she saw her brother, she was going to convince him to come home and away from here, back to a more civilized time.

"Well, since you asked...I'm actually

from the future. My brother and I ended up back here somehow, and once I find him, we will hopefully be going back home."

His eyebrow was almost up into his hat as he listened to her. She had to admit to enjoying the look he was giving her. He didn't believe a word she was saying.

"From the future? I suppose you're also going to tell me you have some kind of magical powers. Or maybe you're a witch of some kind." He stepped forward and turned to start packing the ground around the new post he'd put up.

"If you don't want to tell me, that's fine. Not like you owe me any kindness. But your brother is most likely going to demand I do right by you now since I've held you out here unchaperoned for the past few days. It would be good for us to know a bit about each other before we're married."

"Married! What are you talking about?" Her heart had just jumped into her throat.

He lifted his eyes to look at her, pushing his hat back on his head as he leaned on his shovel. "I'm not sure where you're from, but out here, if a man and woman spend any time together, her reputation is ruined. So since you don't have anyone else to step up and marry you, it will be my duty."

"Your duty? Are you serious? I'm not marrying you. I don't even know you. And I certainly am not marrying a man who kidnapped me. What would have happened to the poor woman you were supposed to be taking? Would Martin still have gone through with marrying her after she'd been with you like this? You people back here have some strange rules. Even though it isn't the woman's fault whatsoever, she's still punished by having to marry the man who actually ruined her reputation. I seriously feel bad for women in this time."

"Right, I forgot you weren't from this time." He rolled his eyes as he crouched down to give Mollie a pat on her head as she pushed into his leg. "I assume Martin would have still married her, not wanting me to have anything he felt was rightfully his. But if he hadn't, I guess I'd have had to step up and do right by her too."

She could only shake her head as she stared at him. "You really hadn't thought any of this through, had you?"

He was carefully pulling a piece of the fabric back to look at Mollie's leg since she was standing by him. He shrugged. "I really hadn't expected quite so many complications. I'd hoped to send a message to Martin the next day, but then the whole Mollie incident happened. And then, I find out I don't have the right woman anyway."

She watched him gently check the wound on the leg, whispering to Mollie the whole time, who quite obviously trusted him completely. Her head was down with her nose resting on his hat.

"You should be glad you had the wrong woman. At least you might not get into so much trouble for your crime. I doubt my brother will press charges once I explain everything to him."

His eyes lifted and met hers. "What about you? Don't you want to see me pay?"

Her heart did a strange flutter as she kept her gaze on his.

"No, I don't think you're a bad man. You just haven't made good decisions, that's all."

The side of his lip curled up into a half smile. "Well, you're likely the only person who would say I'm not a bad man, Charlotte."

Something in the way he said it made her feel a sadness for him. She tilted her head, as she crossed her arms over her chest, resting her elbows on her knees.

"Why do you still insist on calling me Charlotte? I've told you just to call me Charlie like everyone else does."

He shook his head. "I can't. Charlotte

is a beautiful name, and it belongs to a beautiful woman. Charlie doesn't suit you."

Her mouth opened, but she didn't know what to say. In all her life, she'd never had anyone tell her she was beautiful in such a sweet way. And coming from a man like Gabe had shocked her to the core.

He was already looking down and tying up the bandage on Mollie's leg, not even realizing how much he'd just set her heart racing.

She suddenly realized she needed to get away from him as soon as she could. She wasn't afraid of him hurting her—she hadn't been afraid of that since the day she'd got here. He wasn't the type of man who'd hurt a woman physically. Of that, she had no doubt.

It was the other kind of hurt he could do to her that scared her.

She couldn't fall for a man in another time. Not him.

But as she watched him stand back up, giving Mollie a scratch under her neck before the foal ran back to her mother, she realized that she was dangerously close to letting that happening.

Chapter 12

*H*e raced to the cabin, his heart in his throat as the smoke billowed from the front door and windows. If he thought he was in trouble after abducting the wrong woman, he'd be sure to face the firing squad if he let her get burned to death.

"Charlotte, where are you?" He pushed the door open completely, choking on the smell in the small room.

He could hear her coughing, and moved toward the sound. "I'm over here. I'm fine."

He stopped when he got closer to her by the stove, and he suddenly realized where all the smoke was coming from. There was a pan on top of the stove's grate, with something inside the color of dirt.

She stood there looking down at it with a distressed look on her face, and he had to pull himself together not to laugh out loud. The house wasn't on fire. She was just trying to cook.

"You've been busy fixing up the pen, and since you're taking me to my brother tomorrow, I thought I'd do something for you. You haven't been completely horrible to me, as far as kidnappers go, so I was going to show you there are no hard feelings." He could hear shock in her voice, as though she didn't know whether the fact she was making a meal for her kidnapper was unbelievable, or the fact that she'd actually thought she could cook.

"Well I appreciate the effort." He was doing his best not to let a smile reach his face, and was glad he'd pulled it off when she looked up at him.

"I'm actually not a bad cook. I've just never cooked on a stove like this before, with real fire."

"It's a pretty old stove, so I'm sure the ones you would be used to in the city are much more modern."

He'd never had anyone try to do something nice like this for him before, so he wanted her to know he did truly appreciate the effort. Even if the results staring back at him in the pan were completely inedible. But he was going to have to try.

He reached out and took a blackened piece between his fingers, bringing it up to his mouth. Taking a deep breath, he put it in and tried to chew. It completely disintegrated in his mouth into charcoaled ash, making him choke. He rushed over to grab the dipper out of the water bucket and took a long drink.

When he could talk, he looked back through the smoky room to see her standing watching him with one eyebrow raised. "It wasn't bad bacon. A little overdone, but really not too bad at all."

His throat was still dry and scratchy so he took another quick sip of water. She still stood watching him, wearing his oversized clothes that were hanging off her, with soot on her face and her hair falling in a disheveled mess around her face.

And yet, he was sure he'd never seen a woman look so wonderful and feminine.

When she smiled and started to laugh, his chest clenched with a strange emotion.

"It wasn't bacon. I'd cut up some potatoes to fry, but wasn't quite sure how to do it using this." Her voice was full of laughter as she waved her hand to indicate the stove.

"That was a potato?" He couldn't even keep the surprise from his voice as he started to choke again.

She was laughing hard now, clenching her stomach with her arms. "I think we might have to get takeout."

"I'm not sure what that is, but I do know I need some fresh air. How about if I just do some bacon over the open fire tonight and we let the cabin air out a bit?"

She was already moving to the front door, waving her arms to get the smoke from her eyes as she went.

"You won't get any argument from me."

***

The smoke from the cabin, combined with the smoke from the fire they sat around, still filled her nostrils. She was desperate for a shower, or at least some warm water she could bathe in. At this point, she'd even be willing to go splash around in the creek that ran behind the barn, as long as she had some soap.

"So, how do you keep yourself clean?" Gabe always had a bit of scruff around his jaw, but other than that, she realized he was always washed. She'd always imagined people back in the pioneer days, before running water probably smelled less than fresh. Yet Gabe had a smell that reminded her of leather and musk, and was in no way offensive. It was a scent that was unique to him.

He was putting the last of his bacon into his mouth, and he looked up at her with a shocked expression. She supposed she could have tried to not be so blunt, but the simple truth was—she needed to get clean again.

"I beg your pardon?" He slowly reached down and set his tin plate on the ground beside him. He was sitting on an overturned log, and the fire illuminated his face with a soft orange glow.

She'd insisted they build the fire near the house, because of her fear of the watchful eyes out in the darkness beyond the yard. But she was still keeping a close watch on the brush surrounding them just in case.

"Well, I've been here for a few days, and I'm desperate for a good wash. At this point, I'd even be willing to bathe in the creek if I have to. However, I'd prefer at least some warm water, and the safety of four walls around me if I could."

He clenched his eyes closed tightly and pushed his hands up under his hat, moving it back on his head. Air hissed between his teeth. "I never even thought about that. I'm so sorry."

He jumped up from the log, and strode toward the cabin. Charlie scrambled to get off the ground and follow him. She wasn't about to be left out here in the dark by herself.

"Where are you going?"

He stopped suddenly, and she ran into the back of him. As he turned, he grabbed her arm to stop her from falling over. "You said you wanted a bath. I'm going to get you some water from the creek, and I'll warm it on the stove for you. I'm afraid I normally just wash right in the creek, but I never thought that a lady might like a little more comfort."

She was having a hard time concentrating on what he was saying as he held her arm, keeping her close to him as he spoke. Pulling her arm free from his grip, she took a step back away from him.

"I didn't mean right now. I can wait until morning."

His eyes stayed on hers. "I really am sorry, Charlotte. I should have been more thoughtful to your needs, especially since you never asked to be dragged out here in the first place." He pushed his hand back through his hair again, then pulled his hat down hard.

She felt bad seeing the remorse he had in his eyes. "It's not like I have any clean clothes to change into anyway." She tried to laugh and let him know she was joking.

But his serious expression showed her the extent of the guilt he was feeling.

"I'll get the tub out in the morning and fill it with warm water for you. It's small, but I think you'll fit in it just fine. And I'll find some clean clothes for you to wear until we can get you to your brother. I can just imagine his reaction when he sees what you're wearing. I'll be lucky to come out of that meeting with my head still attached to my body."

"I can handle my brother. I'll be sure to make certain he doesn't cause you too much harm." She offered him a smile, knowing how nervous he probably was about the confrontation he was sure to have with him tomorrow.

They stood facing each other, their gazes locked together as the moonlight offered a glimmer of brightness between them. The crackling of the fire was behind them, then she jumped, landing against his chest as the sound of a howling wolf tore through the silence. It sounded like it was right behind her too.

Thankfully, it was still dark enough that he wouldn't be able to see the burning she could feel in her cheeks as his hands steadied her in front of him. He looked down at her with eyes reflecting the firelight behind her. He hadn't let go of her arms, and as much as she knew she needed to step back, her legs had suddenly turned to lead. Her breath caught in her chest as the beating of her heart started to sound in her ears. She could feel his chest moving as he breathed against hers.

She told herself it was fear from the wolf in the mesquite, but no matter how hard she tried to convince herself, she knew the truth.

Gabe stepped back, dropping his hands to his side. He reached up and pulled down on the front of his hat, nodding his head as he stepped to go out around her. "You better get inside. I'm staying out here with the horses again to make sure they're safe. Good night."

Just like that, he walked away, leaving her standing facing the other way. A chill suddenly took over her, without the warmth of the fire or Gabe's body heat, so she wrapped her arms around herself and made her way into the house.

Tomorrow, she'd be back with her brother and all of these feelings she was having for the man who'd just left her would be put to rest.

Just a few more hours, and she'd be free. She should be thrilled to finally have the chance to get away.

So why did that thought leave her feeling so empty?

Chapter 13

"Thank you for the tub and warm water. I will never take being able to bathe for granted ever again."

Her voice coming from behind startled him. He'd been intent on setting enough food out for the animals, and hadn't heard her come outside. He threw the last bit of hay onto the pile and turned to face her.

His breath caught when he saw her standing there in the new clothes he'd put out for her. They were some he'd had for a while. He hoped they would fit her a little better than what she'd been wearing. The shirt was a plaid pattern, and she had the sleeves rolled up and the top button undone. He swallowed hard, wondering how she could not only walk around wearing men's clothes like it was no big deal, but then also leave any parts of her skin exposed?

Any woman he'd ever known would likely have fainted on the spot at the suggestion.

The pants were still too big as well, but she'd used the rope again to tie them and hold them up. They were rolled up at the bottom, with her boots peeking out beneath the cuff.

But the part that stole his breath from his lungs was her smile. The woman was more beautiful than anyone he'd ever seen before in his life. And she'd been put through hell, thanks to him, but still stood here smiling at him and thanking him for something as simple as a warm bath.

"Sorry I didn't have any nice smelling

soap for you to use." He felt uncomfortable being thanked, considering he didn't have any modern indoor plumbing or the conveniences he'd heard tell they had in the big cities. Some places even had indoor water closets. He wasn't sure how that worked but it sounded pretty fancy.

She laughed. "Trust me, I would have been happy with nothing more than warm water to get some of the layers of dust and dirt off. The soap you had was fine." She moved her head to look past him to where Mollie was running around the pen.

"Are you sure they'll all be okay here while we're gone?"

He smiled to himself at hearing her say "we," as though she was just going into town for a few hours and would be back.

"I hope so. It's about half a day's ride to get you to Heartsbridge if we don't push the horses too much. We could likely get there a bit quicker if you can ride as well as you say you can." Something pressed against his leg, and she smiled as her eyes watched.

"I think someone will miss you when you're gone." Mollie was pushing her muzzle against his leg, trying to get his attention. She'd become quite attached to him since her attack, and he did worry about how she'd be when he was gone. But he didn't want Charlotte to worry too.

"I won't be long. Once I get you with your brother, I can ride a bit faster and be back here before sundown." His stomach lurched as he looked back up at her. "If there aren't any problems."

They'd talked a bit at breakfast about her situation, and she'd mentioned that she'd been staying with Cissie Dunham at the boardinghouse until she could take Charlie out to her brother's farm.

That's when she'd told him she'd been carrying a parasol when Hakan had grabbed her from the alley. She'd dropped it when he pulled her onto the horse. That meant it was also likely there would be people out looking for her, knowing she was missing and taken against her will.

"I wish you'd reconsider and just take me to the edge of my brother's property. You don't need to ride in with me. I can find my way if you give me directions. There's no sense in putting yourself at risk. I told you, I'll just say I got lost and found an old cabin to stay in until I could find my way back."

He shook his head as he laughed. "Charlotte, no one's going to believe you just wandered off and got lost for this long. You would never have survived." When she started to argue, he just put his hands up and stopped her. "No, I'm sorry, but I've seen how terrified you are of the wolves around here, I've witnessed your attempt at cooking a meal, and in all honesty, you just aren't the type of woman who could survive in the wilderness on her own."

She squinted her eyes together and

glared at him. "You'd be surprised at what I could survive if I had to."

Something in her voice made him pause as he started to reply. But she whipped around and was stomping toward the cabin.

The woman had more moods than the sky had stars. He figured it was best to just let her cool down a bit before they left. They were both on edge about the trip back to Heartsbridge. He knew why he was so worried about it, but for the life of him he couldn't figure out what had her so upset.

He thought she'd be happy to be going back to her brother and civilization. She could get cleaned up properly and find her own clothes to wear.

But it seemed that ever since she'd woken up this morning, she'd been riled up.

He figured the sooner he could get her dropped off with her kin and get back out here alone, the sooner he could get his own life back. Maybe he'd pack up and leave for good, once old man Templeton returned home.

Maybe he could find his own place somewhere farther west. Yet, every time he pictured it, he envisioned a dark-haired woman dressed in men's clothes laughing beside him.

Shaking his head, he turned to go back to the barn for the last of the feed. He needed to get away from the woman who had taken over his thoughts and was making him crazy.

He'd never admit he was actually going to miss her.

***

"So, you never told me where you came from." His voice interrupted her thoughts as they made their way along the road. The sound of the horse's hooves hitting the ground with each step closer to Heartsbridge filled the silence between them.

"Well, I did actually. You just don't believe me." She smiled over at him as he gave her a slight shake of his head.

"You're still trying to make me believe you're from the future? What is the big secret you don't want to tell me? Are you on the run yourself maybe?" He was grinning at her, obviously trying to ease some of the tension of the moment.

Of course, he couldn't know how close his statement came to the truth.

They continued on in silence, and as each step her horse took got her closer to her brother, the more upset her stomach became.

This was ridiculous. How could she possibly have become so attached to this man in such a short time? The one she had to keep reminding herself had actually *kidnapped* her. She'd only been with him just under a week, and yet for some reason she couldn't understand, her heart was aching, knowing she wasn't going to see him again after he dropped her off today.

It was absurd.

But it was also the truth.

She was sure someday, someone would write a book about this.

"We're just coming onto the edge of your brother's property. My brother was fiercely proud of the land he was going to own someday, and had shown me around it many times, making sure I saw how successful he was becoming." Gabe looked around with a tight expression on his face.

"I'm sorry about your brother, Gabe. You know it wasn't your fault, right?" She'd always sensed anger, guilt, and so many emotions whenever Gabe had mentioned his brother Davis. And since getting to know him the past few days, she realized he took a lot of responsibility onto his own shoulders for things that happened.

He just shrugged, and the muscles in

his jaw worked hard as he clenched his teeth. "I might not have caused the explosion, but I was the reason he was in the mine. It was supposed to be me."

Her mouth dropped. "So, you honestly think it should have been you who died in that accident?"

His head turned slowly to look at her and she could see pain in his eyes briefly before he blinked and gave her a sad lopsided smile. "I do. And it wasn't an accident. Davis left behind a wife and a son. They deserved to have their husband and father around. There wouldn't have been much of a loss if it had been me who died. And it was supposed to be me working that day, so it is my fault. Nothing you say will change that."

She stopped her horse, forcing him to stop and turn in his saddle to face her.

"That's just about the stupidest thing I've ever heard." She noted his shocked expression at her comment, but continued anyway. Just because women may not speak like that back in this time, didn't mean she had to follow those rules.

She flung her leg back over the saddle and hopped down from the horse's back, striding over to where he sat stunned, watching her from on top of his own horse.

"You need to stop always taking blame for everything. And stop believing your own lies about the kind of man you are. You've always tried to make it sound like you're some kind of criminal. Yet even though you may have made some bad decisions, you aren't a bad person. If you were, I wouldn't be riding here beside you on my way back to my brother. You could have hurt me many times in the past week, but you didn't. In fact, you've treated me better than most men I've known in my life."

She wasn't even sure what had her so fired up, and as she stood looking up at the confused look on his face, she realized he probably thought she'd gone completely mad.

Maybe she had, she didn't even know. All she knew was, this man needed to hear someone say he was worth something. She had a feeling he'd never heard those words in his life.

He slowly swung his leg over the saddle and came down to stand on the ground facing her. His eyebrows were pulled together and she could feel herself getting lost in his eyes. They were darker than normal, holding her tightly in their grip, not letting her turn away.

Before she knew what was happening, his hand was on hers and she was being pulled toward him.

Her breath caught as his face moved closer, his eyes never leaving hers.

When his lips met hers, she knew she was lost.

Chapter 14

*H*e pulled his head back like he'd been burned. His breath was rushing in and out of his lungs as he tried to get his breathing under control.

"I'm sorry. I shouldn't have done that."

The woman in his arms slowly brought her fingers to her lips, her mouth half open in confusion. He wanted to back away from her, but he couldn't. His body wouldn't move, as though it had a mind of its own. His hand came up to gently caress her cheek, letting himself enjoy the softness of her skin under his rough hand.

His other hand rested on her shoulder, her hair falling around his fingers.

Her eyes were on his lips, then slowly moved up to meet his eyes. He couldn't look away.

She moved her hand from her lips and covered his, stopping the movement on her cheek.

"I'm not complaining."

His heart stopped as he heard the emotion in her words.

"No, but your brother might." He needed to keep his head. She was his responsibility right now, and he'd already compromised her reputation simply by having her stay with him the past few days alone.

He knew she was likely going to be in

for a lot of accusations when she returned to civilization. And her brother was going to be demanding answers. He couldn't put her in this position.

Reluctantly he stepped back, closing his eyes against the confusion he could see on her face. Bringing his hands down, he shoved them deep into his pockets.

"If you just follow the path from here, you'll be able to see your brother's house on your left in about a mile."

She chewed her lip as she crossed her arms in front of herself. It took everything he had not to reach out and pull her into his arms again, and tell her not to go.

But she just stood there without moving.

"I meant what I said about you. You're a good man, Gabe. Even if you can't see it in yourself. If I was planning on staying here, I wouldn't be letting you run away from me so easily."

He'd never heard a woman speak so openly. Perhaps that was one of the reasons he felt so drawn to Charlotte. She was just so different from other women he'd known. She didn't put on any airs, or act coy. She just said what was on her mind.

And she seemed to see something in him he wasn't sure was really there. Even after everything he'd done to her, she was one of the only people who saw any good in him.

Even his own brother had never believed there was anything redeemable about him.

"I'm not running away. I just think you're seeing something you want to see—something that isn't really there. Besides, you said yourself, you don't plan on staying around here, so there's not much use in saying anything more." He walked back toward her horse, taking her hand and pulling her with him.

"You need to get to your brother, and

I need to get going. If anyone sees you with me, your reputation will be ruined." He was going to help her up onto her horse, but she pulled her arm back, not following him.

When he turned to face her, her eyes were glistening with unshed tears. Never in his life had anyone cried about him leaving. He stepped back over to her, bringing his hand up to touch her skin just once more.

"I really am sorry. I wish I was a better man. You deserve the best, Charlotte."

Her mouth opened, but before she could speak, the sound of hooves thundering across the ground came toward them. She pushed at his arms, and he caught a glimpse of fear in her eyes.

"Hurry! Go, before anyone finds you," her voice rang in his ears as she tried to get him to move.

But he knew he wasn't going to get far. The voices belonging to the people approaching them could be heard already.

"Charlie, is that you?" A man's voice reached his ears, and Gabe smiled at her, shrugging as he stood, waiting for them to stop. Her eyes looked terrified.

"Well, at least I got you back to your brother."

***

She could hear Noah's voice—the voice she'd been desperate to hear for weeks. But at the moment, she wished she could have just one more moment alone with Gabe. She was afraid of what was about to happen now they'd been found.

Why hadn't she just gotten on her horse and gone when he'd told her to? He could have had time to escape when he'd heard the horses approaching.

Instead, they were standing there facing each other, and even though she'd tried to push him away, his hands were still on her arms. And she had no doubt by the expression on her brother's face, he'd also noticed.

Two men leaped down from their horses and ran over to grab Gabe. They pushed him to the ground, and one worked to tie his hands behind his back.

"Noah, tell them to stop. He wasn't hurting me!" She tried to get her brother to hear her, but he was enraged and standing over Gabe.

"I don't know who you are, but you will answer to me. If you've harmed so much as a single hair on her head, you will pay dearly." He finally turned to her, and raced over, pulling her into his arms.

"Charlie, are you all right? I've been looking for you everywhere. Cissie came out and told me you'd arrived back here, but that you'd gone missing. I didn't even know where to look, but I suspected the worst when Cissie said she'd found the parasol she'd given to you lying in the alley."

Guilt that she'd caused him so much

worry ripped into her heart. While she'd been wishing for more time alone with Gabe, Noah had been looking everywhere for her, sick with worry.

Of course, he was going to believe the worst. She just needed a minute alone with him to explain it all. She just prayed he'd listen.

Pushing back from his arms, she smiled up at her brother. "I'm fine, Noah."

By now the other men had pulled Gabe up, and she swallowed a cry when she saw the blood trickling from the corner of his eye. He hadn't even bothered to put up a fight, knowing he'd done wrong. But he'd obviously hit his head on something sharp as he'd been pushed to the ground.

"Tell them to let him go. He didn't do anything."

Gabe's eyes met hers, and he shook his head slightly. She knew exactly what he was thinking—he didn't want her to say anything that would put her reputation in question.

The thing he didn't realize though, was that she didn't give a fig about her reputation back in this time. She'd never planned on staying anyway, and where she came from, things were a whole lot different.

But it didn't matter anyway, because Gabe was already talking. "You caught me. I kidnapped the woman, and held her against her will. Rest assured, her reputation is intact because the truth be told, she's crazy and I couldn't have spent another day with her anyway. I had to stay in the barn the whole time to keep from having to listen to her."

She scowled at him, her eyelids moving into tiny slits she could barely see through. Even though she knew why he was saying it, she didn't appreciate the words being said in front of everyone else.

"Get him away from me before I kill

him with my bare hands." Noah was seething with anger, and she could feel him shaking as he tried to control it. His arm was still around her shoulders, and he turned, pulling her with him.

She quickly looked back behind her as the men pushed Gabe forward. Their eyes met, and she saw him give a slight nod of his head, his lips turned up in a tight smile.

He was determined to be taken away to jail to protect her reputation.

And he wasn't going to let her do anything to stop it.

Chapter 15

"Noah, just sit down and stop yelling. Your sister has been trying to explain everything to you, but you're being too pig-headed to listen." The small woman by the stove came over and set a cup of steaming tea in front of her.

Charlie realized she already liked her new sister-in-law immensely.

Noah had practically dragged her back to his house, and as soon as they got there, had found some of his wife's clothes to wear. The skirt was plain brown, and was a bit too short for her. The cream-colored blouse was tight, and she was afraid she'd rip the shoulders out every time she moved.

But Noah had insisted she wear what was appropriate for this time period. And wearing a man's clothes was not considered proper at all.

A part of her was already missing the scent of Gabe that she realized had been on the clothes she'd been wearing. Shaking her head, she took a sip of the tea and enjoyed the feel of the warm liquid making its way down her throat.

She'd already explained everything to him completely, but he wasn't believing any of it.

"Why didn't you just try to get away as soon as you got there? It just doesn't make any sense, Charlie." He slammed his hand down on the table, getting an angry look from his wife, Elizabeth.

"Noah, Henry is sleeping. Can you please try to keep it down?"

Henry. Gabe's nephew who he'd been determined to make sure was taken care of, even after everyone had treated him like a criminal.

The baby had been crawling around the floor when she'd arrived, and she'd immediately fallen in love with his cherub cheeks and bright blue eyes. Elizabeth had just rocked him to sleep and placed him in his bed at the back of the house, while Noah and Charlie had the chance to talk about what had happened.

Elizabeth sat down across from her and put her hand out, placing it on top of hers on the table.

"I'm so glad to finally meet you. Your brother has spoken about you so often, I feel like I already know you."

Charlie could feel a lump forming in her throat as she looked across into the kind eyes staring back at her. Her gaze moved to her brother, who was watching her intently.

"So, you didn't even plan to come back to say goodbye to me? Or explain where you had disappeared to?" She hadn't even realized how hurt she was until the words tumbled from her mouth.

Noah sighed and looked down at his hands crossed on the table in front of him. "It doesn't work that way. I wanted to say goodbye, but I couldn't go back. If I had, my time would have run out, and I wouldn't have been able to stay with Elizabeth. I hoped you'd understand." He lifted his eyes and looked at his wife. "I couldn't leave her."

Charlie's heart swelled with happiness as she saw the love between the two of them. "But didn't you think I'd miss you? That I'd be looking for you?"

He turned back to her and shrugged. "Honestly? I wasn't sure. The last time I'd seen you, you said you didn't need me in your life anymore and that you had to focus on your life with Derrick. So I decided not to keep trying."

She clenched her eyes tight as she remembered the day he'd shown up, and Derrick had told Noah she didn't need him now. She hadn't stood up to him and had even told Noah she was fine without him. Everything was a blur from that time of her life. She had never meant anything she'd said to Noah. But she was so afraid of what Derrick's reaction would be if she didn't say what she'd been told to say, that she'd pushed her brother away.

And her heart ached that he'd actually believed her.

"Noah, you had to know I never meant any of that. Couldn't you see how much Derrick was in control of my life? I was terrified of him, and didn't know how to get away. I just thought it would be easier not to argue, hoping that someday he'd change his mind and let us be in each other's lives again."

She could tell Noah was getting angry again by the way his hands clenched into fists. "I knew it. I knew something wasn't right. I should never have left you alone with him." He swore loudly, causing her to jump.

"Noah!" Elizabeth jumped up from her chair at the wailing that came from the next room.

Charlie rolled her eyes. She was used to her brother's temper. "Well, it wasn't your place to step in. It was something I needed to figure out on my own. And I did." She didn't want to let him know how bad things had really gotten before she left, knowing it would just anger him even more.

"But now we need to deal with the other situation. What's going to happen to Gabe now?"

Elizabeth walked back into the room with Henry in her arms, gently bouncing him and rubbing his back. "Gabe? As in Gabe Noland?"

"Yes, it would appear that your ex-brother-in-law was the one who actually abducted my sister." Noah had already heard who her kidnapper was, but Elizabeth hadn't been in the room to hear it the first time.

Elizabeth shook her head and laughed. "Gabe Noland wouldn't hurt a fly. He doesn't have it in him. He's always acted like he was a lot tougher than he really was, but that had a lot to do with how his brother treated him. And then how the people in town treated him when he started being accused of things he'd never done."

Noah didn't look convinced.

Charlie proceeded to explain it all to Elizabeth, ignoring the grunts and arguments from her brother as she told her everything.

"It doesn't make sense. Davis was always so hard on Gabe, never believing he was doing enough. He was obsessed with wanting to be successful and having the wealth he wanted, he didn't care who he hurt. I have no doubt what Gabe told you is the truth. If he suspected Martin was doing something, he likely was. But Davis would never have believed him. He thought Martin could do no wrong, and hoped his loyalty would convince the successful businessman to take him under his wing."

Elizabeth shook her head as she continued, "And poor Gabe has been holding on to the guilt over Davis's death for months. It isn't fair to him, because it's Davis's own fault for going there and driving Gabe away that day. He didn't have to go in and work the mine, but his pride wouldn't let his family name be tarnished by his brother being fired."

"You need to tell Gabe that, Elizabeth. He honestly believes everything would have been better if it had been him in the mine that day. The guilt he carries knowing you lost your husband, and that Henry will grow up without his father is consuming him."

Elizabeth looked down at the once again sleeping baby she held in her arms. "Henry will grow up knowing he has an uncle who went out of his way to make sure this farm was paid off for him. And who would do anything for his family, even if he believed they were better off without him." She looked up at Noah. "And he will grow up knowing the kindness of the father who will raise him as his own. A man who understands forgiveness, and giving people the benefit of the doubt."

Charlie almost laughed out loud at the way Elizabeth let her brother know in no uncertain terms that he had to listen to his sister, and believe her when she said Gabe had never hurt her.

Now, if she could just convince the judge and the rest of the community of Heartsbridge that Gabe Noland wasn't the criminal they all believed him to be.

Chapter 16

He wasn't sure how, but Hakan had already heard about his arrest, and had shown up to ask what he could do to help. For a man who was good at staying in hiding, he sure always seemed to be close by, seeming to know everything that was going on around him.

"So, I hear your lady captive was wearing your clothes when they found you."

"Why am I not surprised you've

already heard every detail?" Hakan had been Gabe's only friend, and even though they had different cultures and backgrounds growing up, it hadn't ever come between them. When everyone else believed the worst of Gabe, Hakan had never turned his back.

They'd met years ago when they were kids, and had never told anyone about the other. Through the years, they met up now and then, and always seemed to know when the other was in need of friendship.

Hakan shrugged. "So, why don't you just tell them it was me who grabbed the lady?"

Gabe put his arm up over his forehead. He was lying on the cot in the small cell, waiting for his turn before the judge. He hadn't expected any visitors, although he should've known Hakan would somehow find out what had happened.

"Doesn't matter. You were only doing it for me. And I could have taken her straight back to her brother. I was the one who dragged her all the way to my cabin and forced her to stay there with me."

"From what I heard, she might not have been forced at all."

Gabe sat up quickly, throwing his legs over the side of the cot. He stood and walked over to the bars between them where his friend stood grinning.

"How'd you hear something like that?"

Hakan laughed. "I have my ways."

Gabe thrust his fingers through his hair, angry that there was already the possibility of Charlotte's reputation being brought into question.

"Look, just let me deal with everything here. I need you to get to the old man's cabin and check on the livestock. I'm worried about the wolves coming back. A foal was attacked the other night, and I'm sure they won't just give up, even though I did try to make everything more secure before I left."

"Well, since I guess I owe you again for not mentioning my part in the crime, I can go that way and look in on everything. I'm sure we both know what would happen if you had told them I'd grabbed the woman from the street. They'd hang me first, then ask questions."

The men spoke in hushed voices, not wanting Sheriff Stanton to hear them. The sheriff had been fair in his treatment of Gabe, and as they had talked a bit taking his statement, they'd realized they both had a strong dislike for Martin Paine.

Of course, he'd also told Gabe he'd gone about things the wrong way, and should have come to the law if he had suspicions about the man or felt he'd been swindled out of money.

"Do you think the woman will say anything about me?"

Gabe shook his head. "No, in fact, I'm more worried she will say something to get herself in trouble."

Hakan smirked at him through the bars. "I figured you'd have your hands full with that one. What I don't get is, why don't you just tell the truth and let them know you'd realized you made a mistake in kidnapping her and were planning to return her once you were able? And that in truth, she was free to leave at any time?"

"Because if I do that, her reputation will be ruined. Her chance of ever marrying or finding a man to treat her the way she deserves will be gone. Besides, just because she was free to leave, doesn't mean she could have even if she'd wanted to. I may have mentioned the wolves that could tear a woman limb from limb if they came across them on their own. Once she knew that, she'd never have even tried to go anywhere without someone to protect her."

He cringed inwardly as he listened to

Hakan laugh. He hadn't really lied to her—the wolves around here were dangerous this time of year when they were hungry. But she'd have likely been all right if she'd stayed on the path and on her horse.

Why hadn't he just let her go when he'd realized his mistake? He could have given her directions for her brother's place, and been done with her.

Instead, he'd found reasons and excuses to make her stay.

He knew exactly why, and the thought fell upon him like a thousand bricks as he watched his friend leave the building. Hakan was shaking his head and still laughing as he made his way out onto the street.

Gabe moved back to sit on the cot. Resting his elbows on his knees, he leaned forward to put his head in his hands.

He'd spent a week with a woman, and somehow she'd managed to work her way under his skin. The strange thing was, she'd done it while wearing men's clothes and not even trying to be flirtatious with him in the least. In fact, he still believed she was perhaps a bit crazy, but it didn't stop his heart from beating twice as fast when he thought about her.

Maybe it was him who'd slipped a cog, leaving him with the belief he could have fallen for a woman like her.

"Looks like you got some more visitors. You're a popular man." Frank Stanton's voice at the edge of his cell made him jump, whipping his head up to see who could possibly be coming to see him now.

"Sheriff Stanton, could we take a moment to talk with you?" Charlotte's eyes met his, and he suddenly had a bad feeling.

"What are you doing here?" he ground the words out between clenched teeth, hoping she'd turn and leave before doing or saying anything.

"I've missed you too, Gabe," the

words were said sarcastically as she rolled her eyes in his direction before turning to face the sheriff. Her brother stood beside her, and the glare he was shooting in Gabe's direction left no doubt in his mind that Noah wasn't happy Charlotte was here either.

"I'm just wondering what day Gabe's trial will be? I've been told there isn't a judge here all the time, so wanted to see how long it will be until he arrives."

The sheriff looked stunned, as though he'd been expecting Noah to do the talking, and was shocked that a woman had been so forward.

It could also be the fact that Charlotte was standing there looking stunning in a simple long skirt made from pink fabric so pale it was almost white. She wore a matching blouse, and he immediately noticed she'd actually done all of the buttons up to the top. Her black hair was done up in a high bun, with tendrils of curls hanging down around her face.

If he hadn't noticed how beautiful she was before, his breath was completely taken away now.

"Um…may I ask who you are, ma'am? I can't just be giving information out to complete strangers who come walking in the door." The sheriff quickly glanced in his direction, then back to Charlotte.

"I'm Charlotte Langley. The woman this man abducted. I want to find out exactly what his charges will be, and his possible sentence."

Sheriff Stanton swallowed hard. He moved his eyes to Noah, who put his hand out to shake it. "I'm Noah Langley, her brother."

"Well, I'm not quite sure what to tell you. The charges of kidnapping are serious."

"What if it were to be revealed that I wasn't actually kidnapped, or held against my will?"

Sheriff Stanton's eyes narrowed

suspiciously. "Well then, ma'am, I suppose there wouldn't be anything to hold him on for those charges. However, Martin Paine has also pressed charges against him for theft from the mines, so he'd still have to go before the judge for those charges."

"That's absurd! What kind of proof does he have that anything was stolen from him?"

The sheriff shrugged. "I'm not rightly sure, but I know he said he'd bring the proof to the trial."

Gabe almost laughed out loud at the expression on her face. "What kind of justice system do you people have here? You can arrest a man and hold him without even having any proof?"

"Charlotte, just drop it. I will face the judge tomorrow, and hopefully he'll be able to see through Martin's lies." He made sure her eyes met his before continuing, "As for the other charges, I will do the time required for the crime I committed."

"Ma'am, did this man abduct you and hold you against your will?" The sheriff was looking back and forth between them, waiting until she faced him again. "And remember, your reputation could suffer irreparable damage if it were to be revealed you had gone willingly."

Even the sheriff knew what she would be faced with if she said she hadn't been held against her will.

"I don't care about my reputation. I don't plan on staying here long anyway." She brought her eyes back to Gabe's. "I went with Gabe Noland willingly, and stayed with him by my own choice."

Chapter 17

*T*hey spoke with the sheriff, and asked for his discretion, mentioning they'd rather the truth not come out until the trial. Since Gabe was still going to have to be held until he faced the judge, Sheriff Stanton agreed. He'd said that only the judge could drop the charges anyway, so she'd have to speak to Judge Thornton at the trial.

"You know you're going to have to marry him now, don't you?" Noah's voice cut through her thoughts.

They were sitting in the dining room at Cissie's, where they'd decided to stay for the night until the trial the next day. The afternoon sun shone in the windows, reflecting off the dust that hung in the air outside.

She turned back to face her brother who sat across the table from her. "No, I won't. My reputation won't matter here when I go back home."

Cissie was sitting beside her, and she reached out and placed her hand on Charlie's arm. "Are you going back for sure?" she spoke the words quietly, without judgment.

Charlie looked out the window at the dust filled street. People were walking along the wooden walkway, coming in and out of the run down looking buildings. Horses walked past with riders on their backs, and pulling wagons filled with families and supplies.

Everything looked hot, dirty, and old.

But then her eyes made their way to the sheriff's office at the far end of the street, and she pictured the man sitting behind the walls.

"I honestly don't know how I can stay here. Everything is so different from what I'm used to."

"It takes some getting used to, that's for sure, but what do you have to go back for? You know Mom has moved on with her life, and we don't fit in that anymore. And I can't go back. You'd be all alone."

She turned to look at her brother. "But how can I stay here? I've become so accustomed to having the technology and the modern conveniences. I honestly just don't think I can survive much longer without proper toilet paper." She knew she was being petty, considering leaving her only family to go back to her own time because she couldn't stand having to use an outhouse.

"What? You don't like splinters in your toilet paper?" he teased her.

She raised her eyebrows at him sarcastically.

"And what about my phone? Cars? Even medicine…you know how much more chance we have of surviving something in our own time. I just don't know if I can give it all up."

Cissie pulled her pocket watch out and looked down at it. It was exactly the same as the one Charlie had seen Moira holding.

"I'm afraid you'll need to decide soon. The hands are slowing down."

"What do you mean? How much time do I have to decide?"

Cissie shrugged. "I can't be sure. Not long—a day, maybe two."

Suddenly her throat filled with a dryness that threatened to choke her. She reached out and took a sip from the water glass in front of her.

"I don't know what to do." Her eyes found her brother's. "I don't want to leave you, but I don't know if I can live here."

And what would happen if she did stay here? She'd just destroyed her reputation by telling the sheriff she'd gone with Gabe willingly. He wouldn't be happy being tied to her, having to get married to protect her name.

This time, Elizabeth reached out to take her hand. "I know things are different here than you're used to. I've had to watch your brother go through so much to get accustomed to life here. But I know he misses you, and I'm sure you've missed him too. If you stay, I promise to do my best to help you learn how to make the best of things in this time."

Charlie smiled at her sister-in-law. Noah had truly found a good woman to spend his life with. She was sure he'd made the right decision in staying here, and would never miss what he'd left behind.

Could she do the same if she had someone to love, and who loved her in return? What if that never happened for her here?

She didn't know if that was a risk she was willing to take.

***

"Hello, Mr. Paine. You have no idea how happy I am that you agreed to meet with me." Charlie stuck her gloved hand out for him pull it up to his lips to press a soft kiss to the back.

She tried not to let the distaste show in her face as he smirked at her.

"I was happy to hear from you, Miss Langley. What a dreadful situation you were put in at the hands of that heathen, Gabe Noland. I feel horrible that you were taken as a means to punish me, especially when you had no involvement at all. Thankfully, my own sweet Clara has been delayed and still hasn't made it out here, so she's safe from the hands of that monster."

Charlie bit her tongue at the fact the poor, sweet Clara would be walking into the hands of an even bigger monster.

She pulled the fan out that Cissie had lent her, and started to wave it around her in a show of trying to cool herself down. "My, it's so hot out today. After the horror I've endured, I find myself not being able to stand the heat as much. Would you mind terribly taking me for a walk outside to get some fresh air, so we can get to know each other a little better? I have so much to thank you for, knowing you're the one who's making sure that man goes to trial for his crimes." She felt sick even saying the words, and seeing the leer in his eyes as he looked at her.

His dear, sweet Clara obviously wasn't the only woman he believed he could have showing him affection. And he was loving the attention Charlie was giving him.

They stood in his office, and as she looked around at all of the cabinets full of papers, she knew there would have to be something in there that would have some answers.

They walked into the small lobby outside his office, and he turned to lock the door. He'd bragged around town about the new combination lock he'd acquired that had only been invented a few years prior. In his opinion, no one could break into his office with the newest technology protecting it.

"Oh dear, I've forgotten my parasol sitting beside the chair in your office." She brought her hand to cover her lip in feigned dismay.

"It's no trouble, Miss Langley. I will get it for you."

Martin reached back for the lock and started turning the tumbler. She knew he'd never think a woman would be able to understand how the tumbling lock system worked, however he didn't realize how much further things had advanced by Charlie's time.

As she pretended to fan herself and look disinterested, she carefully took note of the combination and how many times they were turned.

He pulled it back open then smiled to her as he went back into his office. She quickly grabbed a pencil off the small desk out front, and wrote the combination on a piece of notepaper, then made sure to fold it and place it tightly in her hand.

By the time he came back out, she was standing and smiling sweetly in his direction.

"Thank you so much. I daresay I'd have burned my skin out in this sun without my parasol as cover."

As they walked into the heat of the air outside, Charlie smiled to herself. Out of the corner of her eye, she saw the person she was looking for, and discreetly dropped the now crumpled up paper to the ground.

Martin always bragged to anyone who would listen how he would never let anyone take something that belonged to him.

He was about to find out how wrong his arrogance was.

Chapter 18

Sheriff Stanton walked beside him as they made their way to the municipal office where Judge Thornton would be listening to the cases today. Gabe kept his head up, not making eye contact with the people of the community who'd already convicted him in their minds.

It was the same as it had always been. They'd believed the lies Martin Paine had spread about him before, and had already found him guilty of the latest crimes.

People stopped to watch, whispering

to each other as they continued up the street.

"Don't pay these people any mind. Most of the town already know Martin Paine isn't an honest man, so I have no doubt they can almost understand the reasoning behind your crime. I'm sure they've all heard why you grabbed the woman in the first place, and while they might not condone what you did, I'm sure most of them can understand your frustration."

Frank Stanton walked holding his hands on his gun belt, making sure everyone knew he wouldn't tolerate any threats to him or the prisoner. For an older man he was still surprisingly tough, and didn't take any guff from anyone.

"Unfortunately, a lot of these people have heard things about me for many years, and I'm certain their trust in me is long gone. I don't expect any loyalty from any of them."

Just as they were getting to the front steps of the building, Gabe's eyes found a couple walking up the street toward them from the other direction. The hair on the back of his neck stood on end when he realized it was Martin Paine and a woman with a large hat, her head tipped down as she strolled along with her arm entwined in his.

When he said something to her, she laughed, lifting her head so Gabe could see her face. His eyes met the hazel eyes that had taken over his dreams at night, the eyes that changed color with her moods.

What was Charlotte doing with that monster?

His chest clenched as jealousy consumed him. After everything she'd heard about that man, why would she be enjoying a walk with him and letting him escort her to his trial? She'd already told Sheriff Stanton she didn't want charges to be pressed against Gabe, and that was going to be coming out during the trial.

He didn't think Martin would take that news well. Especially when he realized he'd escorted a lady to the trial who would, in the eyes of the world around her, be considered a fallen woman.

It didn't matter that nothing had happened between them. The fact that she was saying she went with Gabe willingly and spent almost a week alone with him, was going to do irreparable damage to her reputation.

The couple approached him as they made their way into the building. "Gabe Noland, I'll enjoy seeing you pay for your crimes today. I'm glad your thievery and misdeeds have finally caught up to you. And the part that gives me the most enjoyment, is that your latest transgression—the one that finally brought you to justice—was a complete failure. You can't even do a good job of being a criminal. Your brother was right about you—once a delinquent, always a delinquent."

Gabe pulled his arms, ready to knock Martin down with his shoulder if he had to.

The man was grinning as he patted Charlotte's hand on his arm.

"I'm so thankful you managed to get away from that barbarian without being harmed. You will get to enjoy seeing him sent away for his crimes today," Martin leaned in closer to Charlotte's ear, and didn't notice the smirk she wore on her face as she looked at Gabe.

They walked in ahead of them as Sheriff Stanton held him back. "Let him go, Gabe. Men like him aren't worth the time you waste worrying about them."

He had no idea what the woman was up to, but he had a bad feeling everyone was going to find out in a short time. He just hoped she knew what she was doing.

**

"Gabe Noland, can you approach, please?" Judge Thornton had done a few of the smaller cases, and was now ready to deal with the one that had brought many of the townsfolk out to witness.

As he walked to the front, he noticed Noah and Elizabeth sitting to the side. She was holding Henry on her lap, and she offered him a genuine, kind smile. Elizabeth had been one of the few people who'd never thought him to be a bad person, and had always been friendly to him.

Noah, however, was still scowling at him. Gabe figured he'd be the same way if he'd had a sister who'd been held captive by a strange man. It wouldn't be an easy transgression to forgive.

"You're being charged with kidnapping, as well as some accusations of theft. Since the U.S. Marshalls who arrested you were witness to the woman being held by you, there really isn't more proof needed. Do you have anything to say in your defense?"

Lifting his chin, he met Judge Thornton's eyes. He was known as a fair man, so Gabe hoped his sentence wouldn't be too harsh. "No, sir. I have nothing to say."

The judge nodded, then shuffled some papers on his desk until he found the one he was looking for. As he picked up his pen to sign something, the sound of a chair being pushed back broke through the silence.

"Your Honor, the charges against Gabe Noland have been dropped by the victim."

Gabe cringed as he heard the sheriff's voice. He'd secretly been hoping what had been discussed yesterday at the jail had been forgotten.

The gasps in the room echoed off the walls, so the judge lifted his gavel and banged it hard, trying to get everyone back under control. "Silence, or I will clear this room."

Judge Thornton looked out at the people in the room. "Is Charlotte Langley present here today?"

Gabe clenched his eyes tight as he waited for the familiar voice to speak. "Yes, sir, I'm right here." The sound of booted footsteps on the hard, wooden floor reached his ears.

"Is this true? How can you drop the charges of kidnapping?"

"Well, Your Honor, to be truthful, I was never the one who charged him in the first place. I've never really been consulted in the matter at all. If I had, I'd have mentioned that I went with Gabe Noland willingly and was free to leave any time I wanted."

The gasps were even louder this time, making the judge demand the removal of everyone who didn't have any part in the case. The only people left were Noah, Elizabeth, Martin Paine, Sheriff Stanton, and the judge.

Gabe turned his gaze and noticed Martin's face was so red, the whites of his eyes almost glowed. "What is going on here? This man attempted to abduct my future bride, and just because he grabbed the wrong woman, doesn't let him off. Even if that harlot admits to going with him freely," he was hissing the words out, spit flying from his mouth as he boiled over with anger.

"Sir, I'm afraid if the victim isn't pressing charges, there's nothing we can do." The judge lifted another paper. "So, we will move on to the accusations of theft against you, Mr. Paine." He lifted his eyes to look at Martin. "I'm assuming you have some proof?"

"I do have proof. That man complained about everything in the mine while he worked there, and wouldn't do the work he was assigned to do. I noticed various amounts of cash going missing from the small office that is located at the mine for the foreman and me to work out of when we're there. One day I saw Mr. Noland leaving and when I went back in, the box that was hidden in the bottom drawer of the desk was missing." Martin turned to look at him. "That was money that was supposed to be used for acquiring better materials to make the mine safer."

The room fell silent. "That's your proof? You are saying you saw him leave the office, and the money was missing? How do we know there was ever any money there?" Judge Thornton's voice sounded incredulous.

Gabe pressed his lips together as he fought the smile that threatened. Finally, someone who didn't believe everything Martin Paine said was the truth just because he was a successful businessman.

"Well, his brother, Davis Noland believed it as well, and was in the process of paying me back. Here's a note he signed, agreeing to pay back the money that was stolen."

Martin smirked at him as he walked over and handed the judge a piece of paper. Judge Thornton looked it over, then held it up for Gabe to look at. "Is this your brother's handwriting?"

Gabe's stomach sunk when he recognized the familiar strokes of ink on the paper. He nodded, unable to say anything as the realization of just how much his brother had believed him to be a thief sunk in.

It seemed even though he was no longer here, Davis was having a hand in his fate.

"Excuse me, Your Honor. I'd like to bring some more evidence to your attention which we believe will clear Gabe Noland's name, and will prove exactly who the real thief is."

Gabe turned his head to look at the face of the woman who had come to stand beside him. Her face was determined, and even though he was angry with her for not listening to him, resulting in her reputation being ruined, his heart skipped a beat as he took in her beauty.

She may be a stubborn and difficult

woman to understand, but she was also loyal and willing to fight for him. It was something no one else had ever done.

Whatever she was about to tell the judge, Gabe had no doubt she wouldn't back down until he was free.

Chapter 19

C harlie moved aside and let Noah come forward. He placed a folder on the judge's desk. "If you look through the papers in there, you'll find the numbers don't add up from what Martin was being sent from the company who owns the mine, and what he was putting back into the mine."

"Where did you get that?" Martin flew forward, reaching to grab the file from the desk. Sheriff Stanton stopped him, holding his arm.

The door at the back of the room opened, and she smiled back at Hakan. The man who'd physically grabbed her from the street strode forward into the room holding another folder.

"I have something here that will show you the dynamite order that was put in by Mr. Martin Paine. There is a letter from the foreman suggesting the amount was too much to be in use that day of the explosion that killed Davis Noland and the other men."

"What? You have no proof of that. I destroyed any evidence of those orders long ago." Martin's hand flew to his mouth at what he'd just said. He lurched forward, ready to run for the door.

Hakan opened the file and looked down. "Oh, you're right. This is just an empty file. My mistake."

"Sheriff, can you arrest this man and hold him until I have a chance to talk with the witnesses here, and look over the evidence?"

Charlie's eyes met Gabe's, and she smiled at the shock she was seeing in his eyes. He'd tried to spare her reputation, willing to pay the price, knowing people would only believe the worst in him anyway.

And now he was witnessing the man who'd tried so hard to hurt him finally being brought to justice. She had an urge to run and put her arms around him, but decided the delicate sensibilities of the people from this time period would probably be permanently damaged if she did that.

Instead, she slowly moved her hand out to his, knowing everyone else was focused on the scene Martin was creating around them. She felt him squeeze her hand, and their eyes stayed locked on each other, unaware of anything but the beating of their own hearts.

***

"How did you find those papers?" He was still in shock as they all sat around the table at Cissie's. "Martin has always been well-known not to ever leave anyone alone in his office. And it's always locked tight when he isn't there."

Gabe was bouncing Henry on his leg, enjoying the smile the young boy was giving him as he pulled his finger into his mouth to chew on it.

Hakan, who had been leaning against the counter, stepped forward. "Your lady stopped me outside the jail yesterday morning and told me she had a plan. You know me, I can't resist a pretty face."

Gabe slowly turned to face Charlotte. She just shrugged. "Well, you weren't going to do anything. You'd already decided you'd just be the martyr and pay the price for crimes you didn't even commit."

"Have you forgotten I did actually kidnap you?" He couldn't believe he was hearing any of this.

"Yes, but you didn't hurt me. And trust me, that's a huge deal to me."

Noah spoke up from across the table. "Charlie got Martin to take her for a nice long walk yesterday afternoon, while Hakan and I went through every square inch of that office. For a man who was supposed to be such a good businessman, he wasn't very good at hiding his crimes. I'd imagine the law will find enough evidence of wrongdoings to put Martin away for a long time."

Gabe's head was spinning with everything that had happened in the past few hours. Then Hakan said his goodbyes, laughing as he slapped Gabe on the back, telling him he had a good, strong woman, and to let him know when the wedding was. Gabe swallowed hard as heat rose in his face.

Thankfully, just then, Cissie came from the back room, with a tray of tea and fluffy biscuits dripping with butter. As she set it down, she turned to look at Charlotte.

"Charlotte, I'm sorry, but you need to decide. There's not much time left." The woman pulled some kind of timepiece out and looked down at it.

What was she talking about?

He turned to look at the woman sitting beside him. Her eyes filled her face as she looked back and forth between him and her brother. She looked like she was ready to cry.

"Charlotte? What's wrong?"

A tear escaped, and she said, "I don't belong here, Gabe. I wish I could stay, but I just don't know if I can give everything up. I don't know what to do."

He couldn't figure out what she was saying. But before he could say anything, Noah spoke up, "Charlie, it's your decision. But you know if you go, we won't see each other again. We can't cross over a second time. Once the hands stop moving, you have to stay where you are."

Clearing his throat, Gabe brought Charlotte's attention back to him. "Does someone want to let me in on what's going on?"

Her eyes were dark now as they glowed from unshed tears. "I did try to tell you, Gabe, but you didn't believe me. I'm not from this time."

He started to roll his eyes, but stopped as he noticed everyone else around him watching him intently. Henry seemed to be the only one oblivious to the situation unfolding in front of him as he babbled and pulled at Gabe's collar.

His eyebrows came together in confusion. "It's true, Gabe. I didn't believe it at first either, but Noah and Charlotte come from a time in the future." Elizabeth was smiling at him. She was one person he was sure didn't know how to lie.

Slowly turning his head, he looked at

Cissie, waiting for her to explain. For some reason she seemed to be the one in charge.

"Why?" None of this made any sense.

"People get sent here if their heart match is living in a time different from their own. In Charlotte's case, we weren't sure if she just came to get the chance to see her brother one more time, or if there was something more. But when the hands of this watch stop moving, she's stuck here. She needs to decide where she wants to be. The hands have slowed down, and she doesn't have much time."

Elizabeth stood up, coming over to take Henry from his arms. "Come on, Noah, let's give them some privacy."

Noah stood but looked down at his sister. "I'm not going far. Whatever you decide, I will support it. Remember that. Don't go anywhere without saying goodbye."

Surely this wasn't true. Why were

they all acting like it was?

Cissie followed the couple outside, leaving him along with Charlotte.

She stood and paced beside the table. "I don't know what to do. I want to stay here with Noah, and with you, but I'm giving everything up. It's crazy, because you've never told me how you feel, and I'm so confused about what I'm feeling. And I feel so shallow to be worried about giving up things like a cell phone, the internet, toilet paper, and modern showers, but it's just all so confusing."

Gabe didn't say anything, just watched her as she tried working everything out in her own mind. She'd said she wanted to stay with him. That's all he'd heard, and he didn't even know if she realized she'd said it.

"Things are so different here. But if I go back, Derrick might find me, and I'd have to pay dearly for running from him."

"Who is Derrick?" He had a sinking feeling in his stomach.

Her eyes were full of tears. "He's my ex-boyfriend. He won't stop looking for me, and when he finds me I'm scared of what he'll do. I snuck out one night after he came home drunk and pushed me down the stairs. Until then he'd been controlling and demanding, but he'd never hurt me physically. That day, I knew our relationship was headed somewhere even darker. While he was sleeping, I grabbed some money from his wallet, packed a few things and got ready to run." She stopped pacing and looked out the window, as though she was living the moment over again.

"He woke up, and came at me. I grabbed a fireplace poker and swung it at him. He fell, hitting his head on the corner of the mantel. I ran, never even knowing if I'd killed him or not." She brought her arms up and crossed them tightly in front of her stomach.

Gabe stood slowly, making his way to her. He reached out and took her hands in his. He needed to make the pain he could see in her eyes go away.

"He lived, and he followed me. He found me just before I came here, but I got away."

Gabe felt physically sick to his stomach.

"Then you got away from one man who was hurting you, only to be kidnapped and forced to endure even more." His heart ached, knowing what he'd done to her after everything she'd been through.

He dropped her hands. "I'm so sorry. You deserve so much better. I don't think you should go back, not when your brother is here, and that man is back there waiting to hurt you. I hope you find who your heart was sent here to find."

He grabbed his hat off the counter and slammed it onto his head.

"Where are you going?" her voice choked out in a sob, and he almost stopped and turned back around. But he knew if he did, he'd be lost.

"I'm leaving so you can find a man who will treat you the way you deserve to be treated. I'm no better than the man you left behind."

With those words, Gabe pushed the door open, squinting his eyes against the brightness of the sun. Hopping on the horse that had been returned to him after his release, he spun around and galloped out of town.

Charlotte could make her decision, but he didn't intend to be here to find out what that would be.

Chapter 20

She raced out the door behind him, scanning the road to see which direction he'd gone. After the shock had worn off, she'd tried to catch up to him, but he was already gone.

"What's going on, Charlie? Gabe just headed out of town on his horse like the fires of hell were nipping at his heels." Noah came over, looking down at her with concern. "Didn't he believe you?"

She swallowed against the pain in her throat as she fought to hold her emotions under control. "He did. But he thinks I deserve better than him after hearing about Derrick."

Noah looked at her intently. "What do you think?" his words came softly.

She shook her head slowly, but she realized the truth in her words as she spoke them out loud. "He's the one my heart wants."

"Well, what are you waiting for? My sister always was one who went after what she wanted." He handed her the reins to his horse that was tied out front.

Her eyes found Cissie's.

"The hands have almost stopped. Are you sure?" Cissie was smiling at her, knowing already what her answer would be.

Charlie hiked her skirt up and swung her bare leg over the saddle. She didn't care who saw or what they thought. Besides, her reputation was already in ruins, and she was about to go find the one person who could make things right.

She just needed to convince him he was the only one who could do it.

***

She raced behind him, knowing one thing she'd always been good at was riding horses. He wouldn't be able to get away from her.

He must have realized the same thing, because he reined in his horse just as they entered the brush on the far side of town.

Spinning his horse around, she heard him curse loudly. "Charlotte, get back there before it's too late. You said yourself you didn't know if you could stay here in this time. You need to be where you can be happy."

Her chest heaved with exertion as though she was the one who had been doing the running as her horse circled his. "I am where I can be happy."

He shook his head, his horse moving

around to the other side, obviously feeling the tension of the man on her back. "How can you say that? You're running from a man who hurt you, and end up being with another who's no better?"

"You never hurt me, Gabe. I was never afraid with you. I sensed the goodness in you even if you couldn't see it."

She struggled to keep her mare from stepping sideways. "And now my reputation is destroyed, and from what I've heard about this time, no man will ever want me."

She swallowed, knowing she wasn't playing fair, but she knew he wasn't the kind of man to walk away from responsibility.

His eyes pulled together as though he was in pain.

"In fact, I believe you owe me the protection of your name now."

She'd read enough western books and watched the movies. So she knew how things worked.

Their eyes locked, both of them still sitting in their saddles. Suddenly, he threw his leg over and jumped down, striding over to her horse. He reached up before she had a chance to react, and grabbed her around the waist, dragging her from the horse.

She came down pressed up against his chest, her hands on his arms. When she lifted her eyes to him, she felt the breath race from her lungs.

His hand came up and touched her cheek, tenderly making circles on her skin, leaving a trail of heat everywhere he touched. "Why do you make me so crazy?" his voice was strained.

"Everything about this is crazy. I never imagined I'd be traveling through time to find my heart match, and I never would have believed I'd fall in love with a man who kidnapped me, after only being with him for a few days. But that's what has happened, and I know without a doubt this is where I'm supposed to be."

His dark eyes held hers, and she felt his chest moving against her with every breath he took. "How can you be so sure?"

How could she explain to him that in the moment he'd walked away from her, telling her he hoped she found what her heart was searching for, she'd realized it already had.

And she'd do anything to hold on to it.

"Because I know what my heart is telling me. And that is to never let you go."

He groaned as he pulled her in tighter. His lips came down on hers with an intensity she'd never felt before. As he kissed her, his hands moved up into her hair, kneading and caressing every inch, before coming around to gently move along her jaw.

As his fingers barely touched her skin, she found herself scared to breath, afraid he'd break contact.

Finally, he pulled his head back and looked down into her face. Her legs were weak, so she was relying on his strength to hold her up.

"I'm sure I'll never understand how you came to me, or why you've given me your love, but I promise you that you will have my heart forever. You blew into my life like a tornado and have turned it upside down from the first moment I saw you. But I wouldn't change anything. I love you, Charlotte Langley. And I'm never letting you go."

She smiled up at him, placing her hands on his chest. "I wouldn't want it any other way."

As his lips found hers once more, she realized that her heart had been held captive from the moment she met him. And she never wanted to be rescued.

Epilogue

The alley behind the boardinghouse was set up with benches and tables for everyone to enjoy the day. A makeshift dance floor had been put together in the middle, while the sounds of a fiddle played a peppy tune that kept the dancers moving in time.

Charlie leaned in and rested her head on Gabe's shoulder. "Are you tired?"

His arm came around, pulling her

closer to him on the bench. "A little. It's been a long day."

They'd married quickly, before the rumors and accusations could make their rounds to everyone in town. Not that she really cared what anyone else thought, but since it seemed to matter to Gabe, and to her brother, she was willing to go through with it.

She had so much to learn about living in this time.

Martin Paine had been charged with numerous crimes, and even with all the proof, he still denied he was guilty. Many people in town had since come to Gabe to thank him for setting things in motion to rid Heartsbridge of the man they all hated.

After hearing what happened, the company had sent a representative to the mine to investigate further into how it had been run. Gabe was asked to go in and give his input, leading to them offering him a reward for uncovering the problems.

They also offered him an ongoing job as a mine manager but he'd declined, opting to take the other offer that had come in.

"Are you sure you're fine living out in the wilds with the wolves?"

Old man Templeton had written, saying he was staying in the east, with the rich woman he'd found to spend the rest of his days with. He had sent the deed to the property and told Gabe to take over, and make his farm into what he'd never had the gumption to do himself.

With the reward money, they planned to fix up the cabin and make the barn safer for the animals. She couldn't wait to get back out there, even with the wild animals roaming around.

"As long as you're with me, I won't be afraid." She smiled up at him. "But I am going to ask you to build me a more suitable bathroom facility. That's one thing I'm not prepared to give up."

He shook his head and laughed. "You will never quite learn what is proper for a woman to talk about, will you?"

She shrugged. "I will never be proper. And I plan on getting myself some pants and shirts of my own to wear when we're alone at home. I'm willing to do my best to fit in when we're in public, but when it's just us, I'm afraid you'll have to deal with the woman who will never feel comfortable in a long dress."

He tipped his head to the side, reaching up and rubbing his thumb along her neck. "I fell in love with that woman walking around in my pants and shirt, so you'll have no arguments from me."

As his head started to move down, they heard someone clearing her throat. Charlie looked up to see Cissie standing in front of them with a young woman she'd never seen before.

She wore a nice dress, that looked a bit wrinkled from wear. Her hair was a strawberry blonde with highlights that reflected in the sunlight.

"Sorry to interrupt, but I thought you two would like to meet Miss Clara Swanson, the woman who was to marry Martin Paine."

Charlie's eyes widened as she realized during everything that had happened, they'd all forgotten about the woman who was on her way here.

Miss Swanson put her hand out. "I guess I have you both to thank for saving me from marriage to a man like Mr. Paine. I just wish I'd known sooner." She gave them a tired smile as she shook their hands.

Cissie put her hands around the woman's shoulders. "Don't worry, Miss Swanson, I told you that I'd take care of you until we can make other arrangements. It's not your fault you were lied to under false pretenses to come out here."

Charlie watched them walk away, then turned to find Gabe staring at her. "I know it wasn't right what I did, but I'm so thankful I let Hakan talk me into grabbing a strange woman off the street."

"And I'm just glad you grabbed the wrong one." She lay her head against his shoulder and looked out to where Noah and Elizabeth were dancing together.

"No, I think I got the right one."

She smiled to herself as she felt his arms go around her, pulling her in closer.

For the first time in her life, she knew she was exactly where she was supposed to be.

She was home.

Made in the USA
Coppell, TX
27 April 2025